HER SIR & SIRE

By Luna Maree

I0638594

HER SIR & SIRE

Cover by Luna Maree | Edits by Fluffy Fox Publishing | Proofing by Adrianne Normanton
© 2024 by Luna Maree

Content Warning

This book is BDSM themed with strong sexual content, coarse language and scenes of role play non-con. Not all possible triggers have been mentioned. By reading further, you, as the reader, are continuing with the understanding that this book has darker tones and that not all possible triggers may have been mentioned. The author and any who contributed to this work cannot and will not be held accountable for a reader's actions, reactions, or state of mind after reading this book.

OTHER BOOKS BY ME

<u>ALEXIS MAREE</u>
THE KINGS OF HELL SERIES:

The Kings of Hell — Cole
The Kings of Hell — Adrik
The Kings of Hell — Malik

<u>T. MAREE</u>
THE LEAH REYNOLDS SERIES:

Sins in the Silence
Sins of a Daughter
Sins of the Past
Sins of the Enemy
Sins of the Forbidden
Sins of the Blood

STANDALONES

Falling for the Mountain Man

<u>LUNA MAREE</u>

L'Amour Island
Her Sir & Sire

DEDICATION

To all of you who like to serve or be served.

xx

ACKNOWLEDGEMENTS

As always, every book takes a team to make it what it is.

First and foremost, thank you to my family for supporting me and suffering my many hours at the laptop.

Thank you, Rochell Simas, at Fluffy Fox Publishing for your tireless efforts to help me mold my books into what they are.

Thank you, Adrianne Normanton, for being PA Superwoman and helping me to read through these drafts so many times that the words blur.

Thank you to my ARC group and loyal readers!

CHAPTER ONE

I was so tired of being the good girl.

My entire life I'd done what I was told. I got good grades in
school, I went to college and majored in something totally useless
so that whatever man chose to take me home to his family
wouldn't feel threatened by me and the jobs I could possibly
attain. I always looked presentable, I worked out, I kept my head
down, and my opinions to myself when they differed from the
men in my life.

My father had been very good at reminding me that a woman's
place was in the kitchen and at home looking after her children.
A man's job was to see to his family's financial security and
welfare.

Where I lived, people of races other than Caucasian didn't last
long. If anyone tried to preach a religion other than the two
majorities, they were soon asked to leave town. Don't even ask
what happened to people who liked tattoos outside of military
insignias. And if you were gay or anything other than
heterosexual… you would be in serious danger.

Yep. Welcome to my life—raised in a white supremacy
community that liked to pretend they were good, God-fearing
people.

I scoffed and wiped at the wetness on my face.

Even as mad as I was, horribly humiliated and heartbroken, I
could still understand why my fiancé had lied to me, why he'd
cheated.

I'd been driving for well over four hours now. My hands ached
from clutching the steering wheel and my eyes just wouldn't stop
leaking.

And I was damp.

Of course it had decided to pour down rain as I made a hasty exit from my house without looking back. I had no plans, no idea on where I was going or for how long. I jumped into my car and drove off. I guess it was a good thing I had a bag packed with enough clothes for three days. I was supposed to be on my way to my bachelorette slumber party at a friend's house when I'd stopped home to grab my phone charger.

I couldn't make up my mind if I was glad to have caught him or not. Would living a lie be worth not knowing what had been going on? Or was it better to know now before I got married?

I refrained from closing my eyes against the images in my head, and I struggled to hold back the pain that wanted to crash forward and consume me.

He'd cheated on me… with my best friend!

As if cheating on me wasn't bad enough, he had to be so cliché about it.

I couldn't decide which betrayal was worse. My fiancé, the man who I had shared the past four years with and who I thought was the love of my life, cheating on me in our bed. Or the betrayal of my best friend of over fifteen years, my go-to counterpart who was supposed to be there for me no matter what.

I was shaken from my thoughts when a small pinging sound drew my attention to the dash. Shit, I was almost out of gas. I looked back up at the road, squinting through the rain splattering the windshield, and sighed in relief at the sight of lights from a gas station. Even if I didn't make it there, I was at least close enough to civilization to get help.

God—where was I?

I'd never driven outside the limits of my town before, only when I went to college. I didn't recognize where I was at all. While that thought freaked me out a little, at least I was away from home, and far away from everyone I knew. No one would think to look for me this far away. Driving out of town at night, during a storm and alone was *not* something I, Hazel-Maree Connolly, would ever be suspected of doing. Besides, I didn't think Richard, my fiancé, would be so quick to put word out that I'd run away, not after what I'd caught him doing.

I figured they wouldn't start looking for me until tomorrow morning when I didn't show up at any of my appointments. Although—I gnawed on my lower lip as I drove over the town border—I was supposed to be at a friend's house right this moment for my bachelorette party.

I huffed.

Oh well. They still wouldn't think to look for me this far away. I had never been adventurous before; they'd think I was hiding somewhere in town. I frowned. I wasn't sure if I even *was* adventurous or brave. I'd never been given the chance to find out. I was twenty-four, but I had never done anything without the approval of my family before. If I'd ever wanted to go traveling or ride a motorbike, the suggestion would have been ridiculed and the decision taken from my hands. Maybe I *was* brave and curious, a thrill-seeker even.

I guess now was my time to find out.

I glanced around and pulled into the first gas station I found. I was about to get out when an older gentleman stepped up beside me, his uniform showing me that he worked here.

He asked me what I needed and got to work filling up my car. I sat in my silent car and looked out into the surrounding darkness, anxiety beginning to gnaw at me. What was I *doing*? Was this safe? What if something happened and no one knew where I was to help me? Afterall—and I guess I only really had myself to blame—I had no idea how to do a lot of things on my own. I had been raised and reared to be a pretty accessory to hang off my rich husband's arm, to dote on our children, and keep a clean house. What skills did I have to even offer in the outside world? And what was I even thinking?

Yes, my fiancé had cheated on me, and my best friend had betrayed me, but I still had my family back home. I couldn't just take off and never go back because life sucked for me for a bit, could I? But what else was there for me?

I sucked in a deep breath and quickly considered my options. I could go back home to my momma and daddy, but I didn't really want to do that.

The man filling my car tapped on the window and I handed him the cash for the gas.

"Have a good night, love," he farewelled. "

"Wait!" I called, and he turned back to me. "Do you know of a motel or something nearby?" I asked.

"Sure darlin'. Keep going in the direction you was headed, and you'll come across the main strip of town. We're small here, so you won't have to go far. You'll find a place up there and somewhere to eat. But darlin', I gotta warn ya, I don't think this town is for you. It can be a little rough out there," the old man warned.

I forced another smile and straightened my shoulders.

"Thank you for the heads up."

He stepped back, and slowly pulled out of the gas station, sucking in another steadying breath.

Okay, I needed at least the one night away. I would call Momma and Daddy in the morning so they wouldn't worry.

With that decision made, I kept an eye out for somewhere warm and safe I could sleep tonight.

CHAPTER TWO

The gas station guy was right.

This wasn't really my kind of place, but at least it was warm and clean. Sure, the room was old and looked like it hadn't been updated since the seventies, but the door was solid, the locks worked, and it wasn't cockroach-infested. I dropped my bag onto the chair beside the door and checked out the room and sighed. There was a bar across the street, and I could only *just* hear the muted sounds of people and music, even a rumble of a motorbike or two. Geez, this place may be old, but at least the walls did a good job of muting sounds.

Despite the faint sounds from outside, it was still too quiet. I scooped up the TV remote and turned it on just to have some noise. It wasn't like I was going to be able to pay attention to whatever was on the screen anyway.

Was I hungry? No… yes? I huffed—whatever. Looking at my bag, I hesitated whether or not to check my phone. I was sure Richard had tried to call me by now.

Lu too.

The thought of my best friend brought a fresh wave of tears to my eyes, and I sniffed, blinking rapidly to clear them. I would never have guessed… I'd been totally blind-sided…

"Ugh!" I groaned, throwing my hands up into the air. I hated crying.

I stormed into the bathroom and washed my face. After a moment, I decided it was not going to be enough. I felt dirty… used. Mere hours ago, I had lost two of the most important people to me in one fell swoop. Yanking off my clothes, I turned on the shower and prayed for hot water. Internally cheering when it heated up, I waited until the water was as warm as I could stand it and stood under the blistering spray. No matter how long I stood there, some part of me stayed cold and hard... an ache that seemed to reside in both my gut and my heart. My soul felt heavy.

Unable to wash away the bitter taste of betrayal, I turned off the water and took a few moments to squeeze the water from my hair before I wrapped a towel around myself. I caught my reflection in the mirror and sighed. I looked whiter than usual, my pale gray eyes appeared dull and lifeless. My deep brown hair was a soaking, knotted mass down my back. My eyes were a little puffy and red, but that would settle soon.

If my mother could see me right now, she'd shriek at the thought of anyone seeing me in this condition, especially a man. What woman could snag a "good man" when she wasn't looking her best? I scoffed and shook my head. A good man? I couldn't even keep the attention of my *fiancé* and he was supposed to be one of those "good men." What hope did I have of finding someone else? I wasn't worth the effort; Rich knew it and proved it today. Deep down, I think I'd always known it too.

If my father could see me now, he'd just shake in disappointment. Unsurprising, just another person in my life I couldn't please.

Snatching a second towel from the rack, I wrapped it around my hair and made my way back into the main room, only faintly hearing the shouts and calls from the people across the road as they had a good time. Sitting on the end of the bed, I began drying my hair while staring uncomprehendingly at the TV. When my thoughts drifted back to the X-rated scene I'd walked in on this afternoon, I slammed my eyes shut and threw the towel angrily.

Shit.

I was going to go crazy sitting here doing nothing. Someone across the road shouted again and another round of raucous laughter sounded. Maybe I could have a couple of drinks? Maybe dance a little? I needed to do something other than sit here and sulk.

Was I adventurous after all?

Not giving myself time to think about it, I tipped the contents of my bag upside down on my bed and put together an outfit. The simple little black dress was probably a little too fancy for that bar, but it was all I had that suited, so I ripped off my towel and got dressed quickly. I was reaching for my brush when I caught sight of the ring on my finger. My hand began to shake, and I bit back a curse before I yanked the diamond off my finger and stuffed it into my bag.

I hurried through getting ready, slipped on my flats, and scooped up my purse and room key. I was not going to give myself time to think or doubt myself. I needed to get out of this room, I needed to get my mind off the disappointment my life was right now, and I needed to drown my misery in alcohol. At least I was staying across the road from the bar, so I didn't need to worry about walking far or having to drive afterwards.

The rain had finally stopped, and a cool breeze had taken its place causing me to shiver but ignored it. I'd be drinking soon, and that would keep me warm.

"Are you lost?" a man asked in a rumbling voice beside me as I reached the open door.

I jumped and turned to look up at him... and up... and up. Holy *hell*, the guy was tall. I mean, okay, I was five-foot-four, so almost everyone was tall to me. But this guy was a giant. He had to be six-foot-four or taller, with a wide, heavily built chest and large, muscled arms that were tattooed completely. I followed up the length of him to see a small smirk on his full lips. Several days' worth of facial hair only served to make him look more masculine, and a mane of thick, brown hair sat unkempt on his head. He had a long nose that somehow didn't look disproportionate to his face, and dark brown eyes glinted with amusement.

"Uh… what?" I stammered. His smirk grew into a slow grin, and I wanted to melt. Holy sexiness!

"I asked if you were lost," he repeated a little slower. I blinked rapidly and shook my head, only just noticing the word "security" emblazoned on his shirt.

"N-no. Sorry, I was just coming in for a drink," I answered.

He raised an eyebrow, his gaze raking over me slowly.

"You don't look like you're in the right place."

I shrugged. "I'm visiting and wanted a drink… or several. Is that not allowed for people who don't live here?" I asked, lifting my chin and hoping he bought my false bravado. Honestly, the guy could probably take one threatening step toward me, and I'd be scampering back to my room.

Amusement lit his dark eyes again and I inwardly sighed. The man was gorgeous. Why didn't we have men like him back home? Oh, right. He wasn't exactly white—his naturally tanned skin told me his roots started somewhere else, and people in my community had an issue with that. Another twist to my stomach made me realize that maybe I wasn't as happy back home as I had always thought myself to be.

"Just be careful. You look good enough to eat, and there are some who won't care if you're exactly willing. You get me?" he explained, his expression turning serious.

I nodded. "I get you. Thanks for the warning."

"Let me know if you'd like an escort back across the street when you want to go," he offered.

I frowned, narrowing my gaze on him. "How do you know where I'm staying?"

He smirked. "There's only one place visitors can stay around here, babe. Besides, I clocked you the second you were within sight. Like I said before, you don't look like you're in the right place dressed like that."

"Uh... well... Thanks for the offer. I'll keep it in mind," I promised.

He nodded and backed up a step. I turned around and slowly made my way towards the bar, feeling the eyes of the security guy on me the entire time. I slid onto a stool and let out a long breath, holding on to my courage by a thread. This was not my usual crowd, and I felt like I'd already been warned off. I just wanted to drink away my sorrows and crawl back under my covers and forget the world. Was that too much to ask?

"What can I—woah."

I glanced up and inwardly sighed. Another one? How did this bar have two drop-dead gorgeous men in it when my whole town didn't have *any* men of this caliber? Sure, some of them were good-looking, but they were suit-wearing men, tidy with soft hands. These men... they were... untamed. Raw. Why did that make them so much more attractive?

"What?" I asked when he stopped talking.

"Sorry... you're just not our usual sort. Are you lost?" he asked. I glared. "I really wish people would stop asking me that. No, I am not lost. Yes, I'm a visitor. No, I don't need help. What I need is for you to pour me a drink, and then keep them coming," I snapped.

The bartender blinked at me in surprise and shook his head, a small smile teasing his totally kissable lips.

"Sure thing, sweetheart. What will you have?" he asked. I stalled for a second. I'd never been much of a drinker, and even then, I stuck to wine. This place didn't strike me as much of a wine place.

"Surprise me," I decided. "Just nothing weak or fruity."

The bartender raised an eyebrow but nodded and got to work. A few seconds later, he put a shot glass of some amber liquid in front of me, and a smaller glass with what looked like cola.

"What's this?" I asked.

"Fireball, try it."

I picked up the glass cautiously before I shrugged.

"To forgetting today," I declared.

The bartender picked up a bottle of water and tapped the lid of it against my glass. I grinned and threw it back. Heat immediately bloomed down my throat and spread across my chest. I coughed for a moment, but it wasn't unpleasant, just unexpected. I put the glass back on the counter and sucked in a deep breath.

"Woah."

He chuckled and shook his head. "You aren't much of a drinker, are you?"

I shook my head. He filled the glass up again and I handed over some money before taking a sip of my cola.

"What are you trying to forget?" he asked.

"Nope," I replied quickly. "If I tell you, then I'm not forgetting, I'm wallowing. I want to forget, good barkeep," I told him before I tossed back the second shot glass. The heat was less pronounced this time, and I didn't cough, having expected the fiery feeling. My gaze met his again, and I found myself drifting into dangerous fantasies. He was seriously gorgeous, but it wasn't just the way he looked. This guy had an air about him, something that *commanded* attention. The authority he wielded was... well, it was hot.

My gaze dipped to his lips when he smiled, and I wondered if they were as soft as they looked.

"You know," he began as he leaned towards me, his voice dropping several octaves. "There are other things you can do to forget whatever it is you're trying to forget."

I swallowed hard and leaned in closer.

"Oh?"

His smile deepened and I felt a jolt run through me as his finger traced a small circle on my hand.

"Yes, and I can promise you they will be much more fun to think about in the morning than drinking yourself into a hangover will be," he added.

That tone, the whispered promise of seduction and sex, sent a wave of heat over me. Or maybe that was the alcohol finally hitting my blood stream. But *wow*! I was trying to get over a heartbreak. I felt momentarily guilty... Rich and I weren't even officially over. Were we? I mean, I knew I was done—no way could I go back—but we hadn't had that conversation. Then again... he was in bed with my best friend.

Sex ruined everything.

I shook my head and pulled back, sucking in a deep breath before I flicked the shot glass back over to him. I wanted to believe that this man was interested in *me*, but he didn't even know me. And really, what was there to know? I was a pretty paper cut-out with no original personality. Besides, he probably hit on every new woman who walked in those doors.

"I'll take another drink, please," I answered, avoiding his gaze for a moment.

"Maybe take it easy. You're not used to drinking, and that stuff will hit you hard in a few minutes," he suggested. I glared.

"Another, please," I demanded, slipping more money onto the counter.

He sighed and shook his head. "Eat something, at least."

"I don't see you pestering all these other fine patrons to watch their drinking," I pointed out, my head starting to lighten a little. My lips felt a little numb too and I smacked them together a few times, amused at the feeling.

"I know what these guys can handle. You're new, and you admitted you don't drink much. I'm going to get the kitchen to make you something," he said, not giving me a choice in the matter. I sighed exaggeratingly and nodded.

"Fine, but get me another one before you go."

Instead of doing as I asked, the bartender leaned in close, and I almost swallowed my tongue. There was a subtle shift in the air, in him and it had me second-guessing my demands. I licked my lips as he came closer, his strong arms braced on the counter, his dark eyes pinned to my face causing my heart to race.

"Please," I added in a whisper, for some reason feeling compelled to add the word.

"Much better," he said softly before he did as I requested. He looked over my shoulder at someone and pointed to me and then his eyes. After another second, he tapped the bar and left behind swinging doors I hadn't seen before. I was assuming that was the kitchen.

I shook my head and tried to brush off whatever had just happened. I'd never been good at sticking up for myself when it came to Richard or my family, and apparently, I could now add hot strangers to that circle.

"Hey, pretty lady—"

"Nope." I cut off the big, burly man who had slipped up beside me. "I'm not here for that, I just want to get good and drunk and not talk to anyone. Is that okay with you?" I snapped. He blinked in surprise and then chuckled but tipped his hat at me.

"Fair enough. Take it easy," he conceded with another chuckle before he left. I breathed a sigh of relief and felt my shoulders relax slightly before I dropped my head into my hands and groaned.

What was I going to do?

A few minutes later, I lifted my head to see a small plate of chicken wings sliding up in front of me. My stomach clenched hard, and I hadn't realized until that moment how hungry I was.

"Oh, that smells amazing," I groaned.

The bartender shook his head but gave a soft laugh. "Eat up, and I'll see how you're doing after."

"Wait!"

He turned back to look at me questioningly.

"What's your name?"

"Ronan," he answered after a few seconds hesitation.

"Wow… pretty," I murmured, feeling slightly dazed.

"And you?" he asked, his lip twitching in amusement.

"Hazel," I answered without thinking. He grinned that pristine smile and pointed to my food.

"Eat, Hazel; you need it."

I didn't argue since the smell was making my mouth water. I was sure I was eating less than lady-like, but I didn't care anymore. I was starving, and the wings were amazing.

CHAPTER THREE

An hour or two later—maybe it was three, who knows—I needed to get somewhere quiet. I had been dancing and drinking, laughing with strangers, and playing pool which, I sucked at every time. Someone had dared me to try the bucking bull and I had done it, laughing when it threw me off.

I was having so much fun. And the best part? The bartender had cut me off over two hours ago, which meant I was having fun *while* being sober. Apparently, he was concerned for my health. Whatever. I'd regained full clarity an hour ago, but to my surprise, I wasn't the least bit upset. Nope. All thoughts of my fiancé and shitty best friend were banished. I was enjoying a night with strangers as they taught me to play pool and how to hold onto a bucking bull for longer than twenty seconds. Honestly, it felt a little seductive to get up there on the bull and ride it, but it was also a lot of fun.

I had flirted shamelessly with the security guard. His name was Zakari, and he was stupidly hot. He was also very flirty and friendly, and I had been tempted more than once to ask him to pick me up just so I could see what that was like. Rich had never been able to pick me up like I'd seen men do in romance movies. But Zak made me think he could do it without even trying.

I'd also flirted with the bartender, Ronan, but with him it was like a game. He demanded something from me every time I went up there, and it was usually something that benefitted me—a bite of food, a sip of water—and every time I did it, he gave me this look of approval that just... shit. I have no idea why it was so addictive to have him look at me like that, but it was. It was also a temptation to tell him no and see how he would react. A flash of excitement inside me told me that it might be worth my while to try next time.

I looked up and saw that little door marked *private* and decided to hide out there, assuming it was open.

Crossing my fingers, I sighed in relief when the door was unlocked. I closed it behind me, and I closed my eyes as the noise level died down. The air in here was cooler too, and it felt great on my overheated skin. I let my little bag fall to the floor and leaned back against the door, lifting my hair off the back of my sweaty neck.

"Can I help you?"

I jumped at the sound of a voice and looked around to see the silhouette of a man sitting at the small lounge in the corner. He flicked on the standing lamp, and I let out a relieved breath at seeing Ronan there, one of his legs crossed over the other, his hair mussed like he'd been running his fingers through it.

"Ronan, sorry. I wasn't... I mean... I just needed somewhere quiet for a few minutes," I explained, trying to ease the beating of my heart to a normal rate.

Ronan's dark eyes drifted over me from head to toe and I swallowed hard. That slow appraisal of his eyes felt like his hands were sliding over my skin.

"Having fun?"

I nodded, my voice lost. His smile was slow and knowing, a sinfully sexy curve to his lips that made me want to sigh dreamily. I watched with bated breath as he stood leisurely, his commanding frame somehow seeming so much more powerful now that there wasn't a bar between us.

"W-what are you doing in here?" I asked, trying to get my hormones to back the hell off.

"Taking a break. The music makes my head ache after a while. It's nice here in the cooler air and the darkness," he explained quietly.

I watched his every deliberate step toward me, my knees beginning to weaken. What the hell was happening? Why wasn't I moving? Why did the fact that he hadn't taken his eyes from me the entire time make me tingle all over?

"Do you want me to leave?" I asked, not recognizing the breathy note in my voice.

"Are you still having trouble forgetting what you so desperately wanted to forget?" he asked instead.

I shivered, his words from earlier coming back to me, the innuendo ringing clear as day.

"A little," I whispered, watching the way his eyes seemed to burn at my words. What was I doing? Was I seriously teasing this guy? Was I really letting this scene play out?

"Are you drunk, Hazel?" Ronan asked softly, his voice like velvet across my skin. I shook my head, and he studied me closely.

"You cut me off ages ago. Only water," I answered on a breath when he didn't look like he believed me.

"Is alcohol affecting your judgment?" he asked. Was he closer again?

"No."

"Are you sure?"

"Yes."

"Because you're in a room alone with a man you met only hours ago," he explained.

"So?"

Ronan edged closer still, so that I could feel the heat radiating from his body.

"And I want to help you forget whatever it was you were trying to forget. But I want to do it my way," he added, his voice pitched low and deep.

"Okay," I agreed without even thinking. Honestly, my whole

body was alive with interest and need, reacting in a way it never had to Richard or anyone. What was going on?

Ronan grinned slowly and braced his hands on the door either side of my head.

"Hazel... are you hearing yourself? You didn't ask me how I want to help you forget," he murmured, dropping one hand so that his fingers gently brushed my thigh where the hem of my dress rested. My breath hitched and I kept my eyes trained on his as his fingers stroked my skin, so featherlight I had to refrain from leaning into him.

"I don't care. Make me forget, Ronan," I agreed, suddenly desperate to have him touch me. I didn't want to think about it. I didn't want to analyze if this was a good idea or not. I was still young, and I was truly on my own for the first time in my life. This was the time to be wild and make mistakes and find out who the hell I was.

"You've been drinking," he reminded me, and I could see him closing down.

"Not enough to matter. Make me forget, Ronan. Or I'm going to go out there and ask someone else to do it," I said quickly, meaning it. His glittering eyes narrowed, and his jaw tensed.

"I'll break the hands of anyone who touches you," he growled. I believed him. I don't know why, but I believed that threat. Was it because I had been drinking that he felt so protective? Or was he as interested in me as I was in him and feeling possessive because of that?

"Then you do it. Help me forget," I replied, refusing to look too closely at why I was being so reckless right now, why this man, or what the hell I was even thinking. I just wanted to do something wild, crazy, and adventurous. Something that made me feel brazen and brave.

Seconds ticked by, long and intense, and I desperately wanted to start begging him. But my pride wouldn't allow it, and I felt it was important to let him think. Maybe the alcohol *was* affecting my reasoning because old, boring Hazel would never have let herself be in this position. She would never consider asking a stranger for a quicky in the backroom of a bar just to have something that made her feel alive. I was exploring my possibilities, and I had the distinct feeling that *this* man was the one to show me.

"Spread your legs, Hazel."

I bit my lower lip at the command, a shiver running down my spine, causing my panties to dampen and my nipples to ache.

I kept my eyes trained on him as I did as he said. Approval shone in his dark eyes, and I felt a rush of pleasure at that look.

"You want to forget?" he whispered, his fingers slowly trailing up my thigh, taking the tight dress with it.

"Y-yes." I gasped.

"Yes, sir," he corrected. I blinked and he waited. "If you want me to help you forget, Hazel, then you will call me sir."

Ordinarily, I would have laughed if a man said that to me. But Ronan delivered the words as a command, his voice low and deep, and he had an air of authority about him, a confidence that made those words sexy as sin, and not like he was trying too hard. I had a feeling this man was used to giving orders to the women in his bed, and that they were obeyed.

I licked my lips and watched his gaze track the movement.

"Yes, sir."

Glittering eyes snapped back to mine, and I wanted to cheer at the heat in them. *I* put that there. Me—the woman who couldn't keep her fiancé happy enough to remain faithful—had made this god-like man hot and horny.

Ronan made a *tsk*ing sound and brought one hand to my face, cupping my cheek and brushing his thumb over my lower lip.

"Don't go there," he whispered. "Don't go thinking about what you should be forgetting. Stay here with me in this moment. Feel me, Hazel."

I nodded and my breath hitched when he slid his fingers up my inner thigh, my dress now bunched up around my waist. All that was separating his hand from my bare skin was the lacey thong I wore.

"Do you want me to touch you?" he asked, his voice a low rumble.

"Y-yes. Yes, please... sir," I added, barely remembering his order. Again, his eyes brightened with approval, and I finally admitted I was an addict. Somehow, getting this stranger to look at me like that had become a drug I didn't want to do without.

"Are you wet for me, Hazel?" he whispered, dipping his head so that his breath brushed my neck. I gasped and arched my back, desperate to feel him. But he held back, refusing to give me what I wanted.

"Do you want me to slide my fingers deep inside your soaking wet pussy and make you come?" Ronan added.

I moaned, a spasm of pleasure zapping my core at his dirty words. Holy shit. No one had *ever* spoken to me like that before.

"Please, sir," I whimpered, uncaring that I was begging now.

"Tell me," he ordered. His lips brushed my neck to nip at the spot right beneath my jaw. My eyes rolled back at the tiny sting, and I tried to rock against him, but he kept me pinned with one hand to my hip.

"Tell you?" I almost panted. Ronan raised his head to stare down at me, his burning eyes making my body temperature shoot up.

"Tell me you want me to touch your pussy. Tell me you want me to make you come by finger-fucking you until you scream," he answered, his voice almost a growl.

Oh *shit!*

I closed my eyes, almost coming with the words and the vivid imagery in my head alone.

"Ronan, please," I begged. I gasped, my eyes flying open when he yanked me against him and there was a small, sharp sting to my backside, and I realized he had spanked me. His fingers caressed the tingling flesh, and his dark eyes watched my face carefully.

"Please what?" he reiterated. I swallowed hard, unable to understand the excitement running through me.

"Please, sir. Please, make me come," I corrected, my chest rising and falling with every rapid breath. "Please, I'm so wet."

"Good girl," he murmured, dipping his head lower as he backed me against the door again. Another zap of pleasure to my core at those words and he kissed my neck, his fingers teasing over my drenched panties.

"Oh, sweetheart, you're soaked for me," he rumbled. I ran my hands up his strong forearms to his tense biceps where I clenched the material of his shirt in my hands, needing something real and solid to hold onto.

I moaned, my head falling back to hit the door, rocking my hips against his hands to try and increase the pressure. I was so damn close already.

"So wet, so hot." He murmured with satisfaction, slowly bringing his hand to the top of my panties before he slid beneath them.

"Shit," I breathed in sharply when his thick fingers stroked my slit. "Yes!"

"So fucking wet, sweetheart," he praised and I nodded, rocking against his hand. Slowly he slid a thick finger inside me, and I cried out, so desperate that the smallest touch was bound to set me off any moment.

"Fuck. Do you need more, Hazel?" he asked roughly, and I couldn't help but appreciate how strange and hot it was that I had to call him sir, but he got to call me by my name.

"Please, sir, I need more," I begged, beyond caring how desperate and needy I sounded now. I was well past caring. Sliding two fingers inside me, my mouth fell open in pleasure at being stretched wider, his fingers stroking in a way that had me rushing towards an orgasm.

"You're about to come, aren't you, sweetheart? Come on my fingers," he instructed, thrusting them in and out of me harder and faster, curling them just so.

"Sir," I panted, my eyes closed, my head thrown back and my back arching.

"Have you forgotten yet?" he asked, sliding the straps of my dress down with his other hand, baring my breasts. "Fuck," he groaned and cupped one breast, bowing his head to suckle hard. I cried out and ground my hips against his hand. So. Damn. *Close.*

"Forgotten what?" I panted, my mind a haze of pleasure and need.

"Come for me, sweetheart," he ordered, switching to the other breast. I whimpered, climbing higher and higher, so close to a world-rocking orgasm I knew I'd never be the same. I'd never settle for less than what this man could do to me with only his fingers and mouth.

"Hazel," he said again, a command in his voice.

"So close," I panted, the end just out of reach.

"You're almost there, sweetheart. Come."

I opened my mouth, *so close*, and then he pinched my nipple. That sudden, sharp pinch sent me skyrocketing. Just as I was about to scream my release, he slammed his mouth down over mine, smothering my moan, swallowing it as his fingers pressed deeply inside me. I came hard, squeezing his fingers, my hands clenching his shirt tightly, my nails sinking into his biceps. Pleasure blinded me and my eyes filled with tears as my world rocked on its axis. What the hell was that?

Was that how sex was always supposed to be? Wait, we hadn't

even had sex. That was just him playing with me.

Ronan began to pull his lips from mine, but I speared my fingers into his hair and yanked him back to me, returning the kiss with desperation as I shuddered around him.

He kissed me harder, devouring me while he continued to stroke my clit and help me ride out every little wave of pleasure there was. When we finally pulled away, both of us were breathing heavily and my knees felt like jelly. I watched as he slowly removed his fingers from between my legs and brought them to his mouth. I swallowed hard as he licked them clean, his eyes locked with mine as he tasted me.

"Fucking perfect."

My legs continued to tremble as I panted and tried to come back down to earth. For several long seconds, I stood there, drowning in Ronan's heated gaze. Oh shit, what had I just done? And when could I do it again?

"Do you want something to drink?" he asked, slowly stepping back. I swallowed and nodded, needing a few seconds to get my head screwed on right.

"Be right back," he murmured before he left through a side door that apparently connected to the kitchen.

I tugged my dress back into place and hurriedly shimmied out of my panties and put them in my handbag.

They were ruined now anyway.

Ronan came in a moment later with a glass of water. I took it and watched him as I finished the contents. His gaze seemed to stray to my neck and then to my lips as I licked them. I handed him back the glass and tipped my head to the side.

"And what about a real drink?" I asked. He smiled slowly and put the glass on his desk.

"I'm sure I can arrange that," he replied. I looked him over, my gaze dropping to the bulge in his pants and my cheeks flamed hot again.

"Do you... I mean... Can I help?" I offered, waving towards his obvious erection.

Ronan's brow cocked and he grinned in a way that had my heart turning over.

"You want to suck my cock, sweetheart?" he asked. More heat in my cheeks and I ducked my head.

"I've been told I'm good at it—no gag reflex," I replied, raising my gaze to meet his. Heat flashed back at me, and his jaw clenched for a moment as if he were trying to restrain himself.

"If you could say it in a way that convinced me you meant it and not that you felt obligated to get me off, I might let you. But I can see you're uncomfortable, and I don't want an unwilling woman or one who has to be coerced into sexual exchanges," he explained.

I frowned at that, at the seriousness in his eyes and nodded.

"I do feel as though I owe you... but I'm not certain I want to right now," I admitted honestly. A small light shone in his eyes, but then he blinked, and it was gone.

"Honesty, I appreciate it. No, Hazel. I didn't make you come so you would return the favor," Ronan answered.

"So then... why did you?" I asked, not understanding why he would do it if there was no reciprocation.

"Honestly?"

I nodded. He slowly stood until he came to stand right in front of me again, his height forcing me to tip my head back to keep eye contact.

"I wanted to see you come. I wanted to hear your cries, what your moans were like, how soft your skin was. As soon as I saw you tonight, I wanted to kiss you. I wanted to feel your hot pussy clamping down on my fingers when you came, and I wanted to taste you."

I swallowed hard and my libido sparked to life again. *Holy shit.*
"You really just say it like it is, don't you?" I managed to force
from my mouth.

He smiled and searched my face. "Maybe I like the way you blush
when I say things like that."

I smiled, and his lips curved higher. He was an incredibly
beautiful man.

"Ronan... will you join me for a drink?" I asked. He cocked an
eyebrow, and I laughed and shook my head. "I'm not going to
suddenly start writing your name on napkins with little hearts
around it. But I'd like to spend a little time with you while I'm
here," I added. He smirked and shrugged.

"I'm off for the rest of the night, so I can do that. Do you mind if
my friend joins us?" he asked.

"No," I answered quickly, relieved he said yes. Nodding, Ronan
reached past me for the doorknob.

"Ronan?" I interrupted, and he paused to look down at me. I
leaned up and kissed him softly, biting back a smile when he
kissed me back. He looked at me quizzically when I pulled away.
"Thank you... for helping me to forget," I whispered.

He nodded and I watched the questions jump around in his eyes,
but he didn't say anything.

"I'm going to duck to the ladies while you find your friend," I
told him. Ronan nodded and I hurried to the bathroom.

It was a rare ten seconds where no one was there, so I hurriedly
used some paper towels and water to clean myself up. I felt gross
doing that, but there was no other option. I splashed water on my
face and took a second to look at myself. I had just let a man give
me an orgasm with nothing but his fingers.

A smile snuck out and I grinned at myself.

I had no idea who this girl was staring back at me, but I liked her.

Guilt nudged at me again when my mind tried to track back to

Richard, but I pushed it away. There was no mistaking what I'd seen this afternoon, and I was allowed to do whatever the hell I wanted to get over him. That was my prerogative when he decided to betray me, and with my best friend of all people.

I gathered my bag, ran my fingers through my hair to tame it once more, and then left the bathroom. Weaving my way through the crowd, I made it to the bar where Ronan was sitting. I paused as I reached him, noticing Zak, the security guard there.

"Hey, baby girl," he greeted warmly as I reached them.

"Zak, hi," I said in surprise.

"I'm glad you two know each other. Hazel, this is the friend I was telling you about," Ronan introduced.

This was a little awkward because I'd been flirting with both men hard out all night.

"Let's get some drinks," I suggested and took the seat they seemed to have saved for me.

Between them.

My heart pounding and body more alive than ever, I took the shot glass the female bartender handed me and waited for the guys.

"To forgetting the shitty yesterdays," I announced.

They both smiled and we clinked glasses before I tossed mine back, more than willing to get back on the drunk train.

CHAPTER FOUR

Pain.

Honestly, who the hell was digging into my skull with a drill? And why?

I groaned, my mouth dry and eyes aching. What was going on? Where was I? I frowned without opening my eyes and felt Rich's strong arm wrapped around me, one of his legs thrown over mine. I sighed contentedly, still trying to work out why I had a raging headache.

And then it all came back to me.

Richard cheating on me with my best friend... getting into my car in the pouring rain and driving... going to a bar and drinking... Pleasure... Ronan.

Drinking.

Ugh, drinking.

I worked my tongue again, trying to wet my parched mouth. I still didn't want to open my eyes, my head pounded too much for that.

"You're about to come, aren't you, sweetheart? Come on my fingers."

My breath caught when Ronan's rumbled words ran through my mind, my core tightening at how it felt when he touched me, when he spoke to me. Oh wow... I'd let a man who was practically a stranger bring me to orgasm with his fingers.

I groaned and shifted, only just remembering the arm around my waist.

Wait a minute... if Richard had cheated on me and I had left town, then whose arm was around me?

Ronan's?

The thought was enough to force me to open my eyes. I was glad to find the light in the room dulled by heavy drapes, only a small crack in the curtains allowing for outside light. I turned my head slowly and bit back a gasp.

A very big, very tattooed man was lying next to me.

Not Ronan, though.

Even in my befuddled and bewildered state, I took note of how gorgeous he was, even sleeping. Naturally tanned skin, heavily lashed eyelids, and a full mouth that drew my gaze, and a square jaw lightly covered with stubble. His hair was thick and messy with sleep. The arm draped over my waist was inked up and... did I mention large? I glanced further down, realizing his leg was thrown over mine as well, effectively pinning me to the bed. I noted, too, that he wore a pair of briefs.

Thank God.

Holding my breath, I slowly slid out from under him, praying that I wouldn't wake him up.

Oh God, oh God... Had I had a one-night stand with a total stranger? That wasn't like me! That wasn't like me at all! It had to be the booze.

As soon as I was free from his embrace, I drew in a shaky breath and peeked under the covers. I was in only my bra and underwear. Okay, not exactly ideal... but surely if I'd been having drunk sex with this man, I'd still be naked, right? I obviously would have been too out of it to bother putting my underwear back on if I couldn't even remember having sex, and I couldn't imagine him taking the time to do it for me. I took a mental evaluation of my body and frowned. I didn't *feel* like I'd had sex last night. Surely, I'd know... right?

I glanced back at the man and recognition hit me.

Zak; the security guard. What was I doing in bed with Zak the security guard when I'd let his friend put his hands between my legs in his office last night? What the hell happened? I remembered having drinks with both the guys, Zak was Ronan's friend, but everything after that was a blur.

Whatever, it wasn't important. I needed to find my dress, shoes, and bag, and get the hell out of here before he woke up. I didn't want to have the awkward morning-after talk.

My dress was slung over a chair, my bag hanging with it. Okay, that was good. Where were my shoes? Oh, who the hell cared? I could do without them. I just needed to get out of here.

I quickly slid my dress back on, grabbed my things, and tiptoed out the bedroom door.

Wishing I had time for a drink, I ignored the demands of my body and continued walking carefully towards the front door. I spotted my shoes there and smiled.

Yes!

I was leaning down to pick them up when someone cleared their throat loudly. I gasped and spun around, immediately regretting the hasty action. I groaned and leaned my back against the door and pressed my hand to my forehead.

Ouch, that hurt.

My stomach rolled, and I kept my eyes closed until the nausea passed.

"Trying to sneak out without saying goodbye?"

I slowly pried my eyes open to see a stunning man leaning against the archway of the kitchen. He was wearing an old, gray T-shirt and faded jeans. One hand was wrapped around a steaming mug, and the other was slid lazily into his front pocket. His hair was damp, like he hadn't long stepped out of the shower.

Ronan.

"Uh… yes?" I answered nervously.

The corner of his lip curled into a devastating smirk, but he didn't say anything. I shifted awkwardly and twisted the handle of my bag in my hands.

"Uh... where am I? What happened last night? And why was I in bed with Zak?" I asked, deciding I needed answers. He chuckled softly, and I wanted to smile at the rich, smooth sound of it.

"You don't remember anything?" he asked.

"Uh... not a lot... sorry. I mean, I remember drinking... a lot. I remember dancing, something about a bucking bull, and an incident playing pool?" I replied, frowning.

"Yes, you did all that. Nothing else?" he asked.

My face flamed hot, and judging by the satisfied smirk on his lips, he could see it.

"I remember you and I... in your office and, uh... I remember everything that happened there," I uttered.

"Good. I'd hate to have been so easily forgotten," he replied. I nodded but I couldn't bring myself to look at him. Last night I'd been wild and full of need to prove something to myself. Now I was the real me, and I was mortified by my actions. I mean, the memories are pleasant, but it was *so* not me.

"Why don't I get you some pain killers and I can fill you in?" Ronan suggested.

"Oh, uh... no thanks. I really need to be going home," I answered, searching blindly behind me for the doorknob.

"You sure? Last night you said you didn't want to be anywhere near Richard or your best friend."

I stilled and gaped at him before I groaned and dropped my head into my hands.

"How much did I tell you?" I mumbled.

"A lot... Probably more than you wanted to," he answered. I raised my head to look at him, but his expression was full of understanding rather than humor.

I sighed. "Yeah... well, I don't really have much of a choice. My family will be going out of their minds worried about me. And in the end... it's home, you know? I have to go back sometime."

Ronan nodded slowly and took a sip from his mug. My gaze went to his coffee and a craving kicked in hard.

"Do you want some coffee?" he asked, noticing where my attention had drifted.

"Uh…"

"You can leave whenever you want to, we're not keeping you captive here. But if you want to stay for coffee, breakfast, and maybe even a shower, I won't say no," Ronan offered.

A shower… a hot coffee… I inwardly groaned. Ronan smirked and shook his head at me.

"Here, take some tablets for your head, and I'll get you a towel and something else to wear so you can shower. When you come out, I'll have breakfast sorted," he suggested. I frowned and he cocked his head to the side.

"What?"

"Why are you being so nice?"

He shrugged. "You mean besides the fact that I got to finger-fuck you last night, taste you, and hear you call me sir?" he asked. Heat flashed over me again and Ronan's smile was full of smug male satisfaction. He shrugged and tried to wipe the smile from his face.

"Not all us men are assholes, but you have every reason to be suspicious. Here; unopened and still sealed in its box," he said, reaching behind him to a high cupboard before he tossed me a small cardboard packet. He stepped forward and put the coffee mug on the table before moving towards the bathroom.

"I've drunk out of that cup, so you know there's nothing in it. Take some tablets and have a hot shower. There's a spare toothbrush under the sink. I'll get something ready for you to eat when you come out," he said before disappearing into the bedroom.

When he came back out, he had a pair of sweats and a shirt.

"I don't have anything smaller, sorry," he said, holding out the clothing.

"That's fine, really. Thank you," I replied, glancing up at him again. He smiled and nodded, and I couldn't help but blush. He was a startlingly attractive man, and he was being so generous.

"Take your time," he said, nodding towards the bathroom.

I quickly swallowed the tablets, biting back a moan at the taste of the coffee and hurried into the bathroom. I felt gross, my mouth tasted bad, and I was sure I looked horrendous. I locked the door and glanced around. It was a decent sized bathroom with a monster-sized shower over the huge tub. To the side was a toilet and basin, but other than that, there wasn't a lot more to see. Placing the clothes on the basin, I did my business and undressed. I was raising a leg to step into the tub when I caught sight of myself in the mirror and winced. My eyes had heavy bags under them, and my hair was a mess. I was glad I hadn't been wearing makeup last night or it would have been smeared everywhere.

I made quick use of the shower, inwardly groaning as the heat did wonders to clear my head and make me feel more alive, before I dried and dressed quickly, deciding to just go with the shirt. It came down to my knees anyway, which was a good deal more decent than the dress I'd been wearing last night. There was just no way I was going to be able to wear the sweats; they were too long and the waist too big.

I found the spare toothbrush and scrubbed my teeth and then grabbed a comb I found in the top drawer before I gathered my belongings and left the bathroom. The time I'd spent in there combined with the aspirin had done wonders to dull my headache, so when I stepped out of the bathroom, the smell of food had my stomach growling rather than turning over.

"Is that bacon?" I called.

"You're not vegetarian, are you? I forgot to ask," Ronan replied from the kitchen. I stepped into the other room, and he indicated for me to take a seat at one of the three chairs at a table pushed against the far wall.

"No, not a vegetarian. Bacon is one of the most important food groups there is."

"You *are* the perfect woman," Ronan replied. I laughed and took my seat, stuffing my things down beside me. I turned to watch him work, using the comb to carefully brush my hair.

"So... where am I?" I asked, needing to get some answers.

"You're still at the bar. Zakari and I live in a flat above it," he answered. I frowned—oh right, Zak.

"So, uh... what—what happened last night?" I asked, struggling to get the words out, wanting to know why I'd woken up in bed with Zak but not wanting to ask directly.

"You want to know if you and Zakari fucked?" Ronan asked bluntly. I gaped for a second at his directness, but I shouldn't have been surprised by now. "I will tell you this, sweetheart. If either Zak or I had fucked you, you'd know," he replied, flashing me a wink over his shoulder.

"Okay, I believe you. So... why wasn't I dressed?" I asked, now feeling safer in my questions.

Ronan chuckled and brought a plate over to me with some cutlery.

"You demanded to come up and see our flat. Then you stumbled inside here, shouted a greeting to the flat, and proceeded to toss your bag and kick off your shoes. You demanded that we "get this party started" and ripped off your dress, then you fell face first onto the bed and passed out. It was all rather charming," he answered, taking the seat across from me. I laughed and then groaned, shaking my head.

"Oh, I bet it was. Well... thank you for looking after me. Both of you."

He nodded, and we ate in a comfortable silence, only occasionally speaking. I ate everything on my plate, surprised at how good the food was and how hungry I was.

"Do you want some help cleaning up?" I offered.

"Nah, I got this. You can go make yourself comfortable if you like," he offered, taking both our plates to the sink.

"Actually, I uh... I should be going. My room is just across the road, and I feel like I need to make some calls and sort out my life," I answered, getting slowly to my feet, my clothes in my arms.

"You were going to leave without saying goodbye?" another voice asked.

CHAPTER FIVE

I turned to see a rumpled looking Zakari in the kitchen doorway wearing nothing but his black briefs that did little to conceal the weapon he wielded. He pushed a hand through his hair and my gaze dipped to his tattooed chest and arms, the bulging biceps, and the thin trail of hair that led down his ripped abdomen and disappeared into... nope!

I yanked my gaze back to his, and he was grinning at me in a sleepy, knowing way, and it was sexy as hell.

"Uh, morning, Zakari," I greeted, my voice wavering slightly. Where Ronan had made me feel safe and comfortable, Zak made me very aware of how little clothing I was wearing.

"You remembered my name," he replied with a wink, turning to thank Ronan as he handed him a plate with breakfast.

"Barely," I replied.

He smiled and shook his head. "That doesn't surprise me; you drank a lot last night. But you didn't throw up, so I'd consider that a win."

I smiled and backed up slightly as he entered the kitchen. The room felt tiny with him in it. Ronan wasn't a small man. He was tall, well over six-foot and broad, but he had a different aura about him. He could fade into the background when he wanted to or pull focus entirely. Zak? He entered a room and took up all the space all the time so that it was impossible not to notice him. Zak raised an eyebrow at me and took the empty seat beside the one I'd just vacated, and I immediately felt foolish.

"Well... now that you're up, I can thank you. I, uh... I was not my best self last night. I never drink like that... or at all, really. I appreciate you two looking after me," I managed to say, remembering my manners.

"I warned you last night to be careful, and that you looked good enough to eat. You're just lucky one of us didn't get hungry," he replied with a wicked grin before he took a drink of his coffee.

I almost choked on my breath, my eyes flying to Ronan. A flash of last night came back to me. I had been pressed up against the wall and he had slowly pulled his hands out from my panties and licked his fingers clean.

"Fucking perfect."

Ronan's dark eyes heated exponentially as I remembered, and I yanked my gaze back to Zak, who watched our exchange with knowing eyes.

"Umm…" I stammered.

"I mean, I know Ronan got to be alone with you, a part of me was hoping I'd get the same chance," Zak added, removing any doubt now as to whether or not he knew what Ronan and I had done. My face flooded with color.

"How?" I rasped, not able to get the whole sentence out. Zak smirked, his heated eyes pinned to my face.

"I heard you in the office," he admitted.

I swallowed hard and both guys laughed at my embarrassment.

"So… you and I…?" I trailed off.

"Call me old fashioned baby girl, but I prefer my women to be conscious and consenting."

My shoulders relaxed in relief, but it wasn't because we hadn't done anything. No, it was because I didn't miss it. Zak's eyes on my face were searching, and I realized he probably knew why I'd had that reaction too, and a moment later, his knowing smirk confirmed it.

I swallowed hard as I took that in and then frowned. Wait…

I looked around again. This was a one-bedroom flat, and there were two fully-grown men who lived here. I'd woken up, still relatively dressed, my dress and bag hung safely on the chair. Ronan had said, as if from personal knowledge, that if Zak had slept with me, I'd know it. Ronan hadn't done a thing to make me feel as though I needed to be cautious of him… were they… gay?

Wait, then why would Ronan have… serviced me last night? He was obviously aroused. Maybe they were bisexual?

"Are you two… a couple?" I asked.

Zak sputtered, and Ronan's gaze raised quickly to look at me, his face reflecting shock and confusion.

"A couple?" Ronan gaped.

"Uh…"

"What the hell have you been talking to her about, Ronan?" Zak demanded.

"I don't care if you are. I don't judge people based on who they sleep with," I said quickly, hoping I hadn't offended them or worried them. Although I was judging a little that Ronan had touched me the way he had when he was involved with Zak. Having just been cheated on, I was feeling a little too raw to look at my involvement in that.

"Neither do we," Zak coughed and shook his head.

"I haven't said anything, we just talked about last night and had breakfast," Ronan defended. "And after last night, I'd have thought you'd know I wasn't gay."

Zak looked at his friend in disbelief.

"Then how the fuck did she get the impression that we were gay?" Zak demanded. Ronan shook his head and laughed in disbelief.

"I… you're not together?" I asked.

"No!" they shouted in unison. I bit my lower lip and heat crept up my face again.

"Oh… uh, sorry. I just… Ronan said you both lived here, but there's only one bed, and I figured since neither of you had sex with me…" I trailed off, the heat in my cheeks intensifying the longer I spoke. Two pairs of chocolate brown eyes stared at me in wonder, and I cleared my throat.

"The couch is a pull-out," Zak finally muttered.

"Sorry," I whispered.

"We're not gay," Ronan added clearly, shaking his head.

"Far from fucking gay. I mean, yes, our sexual appetite is a little different from the average male, as is what we like to do in bed, but we're not gay," Zak defended.

"Bi?" I offered.

Zak shot up from his seat and I stumbled back slightly. I got no further than opening my mouth to gasp when he gripped my hips and lifted me up onto the counter, wedging himself between my legs. His hands were on my hips, and I gripped his forearms tightly, trying to hold him at bay. My heart stuttered and I wanted to scream, tried to, part terrified and part turned on.
What the hell is wrong with you?!

"Does this feel like I'm not interested in women?" Zak asked low, his voice deep and rumbling in his chest as he ground his hips between my legs. I gasped at the zing of pleasure and at the hard bulge in his black briefs.

"I…"

"Since I sat down at the table, I have been trying to figure out if you were wearing a bra or panties beneath this shirt. I was picturing bending you over the table and fucking you until you screamed my name. Watching you dance last night, flirting with you, hearing you moan for Ronan when he made you come had me walking around with a hard-on all night. Sleeping beside you while you were half naked and not touching you was the hardest fucking thing I've done in a long time," he added, his dark eyes glittering down at me.

"Zak," Ronan called out, a small warning in his voice.

I was panting now, and a part of me recognized it wasn't all due to fear. My nipples hardened beneath the shirt and a throbbing started between my legs. Zak's gaze heated and it slowly trailed down my face to my mouth. He licked his lips and leaned forward slightly as if to kiss me, and my breath caught in anticipation... or was it fear? I couldn't tell now. Slowly, his gaze raked further down, and I watched his lips turn up slightly at the corners.

"No bra," he whispered.

He heard me and Ronan last night through the office door. He'd known what we'd done, he'd listened, and it had turned him on. I pressed my lips together to prevent myself from saying anything, and dug my nails into his forearms. Zak closed his eyes and groaned slightly. I wondered if I'd hurt him when he rocked against me again, and I realized he liked the small sting. I was intrigued, turned on, shocked at myself, but also worried. I didn't know this man, neither of them. I was pinned to a countertop wearing nothing but an oversized shirt. No one knew where I was or where I had gone...

"Relax, baby girl, I'm not going to force you to do anything," Zak whispered, his lips coming incredibly close to mine despite his words. His fingers had trailed to the tops of my thighs, tracing small circles where the shirt was barely covering everything important.

"You have me pinned to the counter, what else am I supposed to think?" I asked, my voice shaky and breathless. I tried not to like the way he called me *baby girl,* but it was a useless effort. And him forcing me wasn't what was really worrying me, it was that he wouldn't *have* to force me. I was so turned on; I didn't know how to react.

"If I had wanted to take you, I could have last night. I am not interested in an unwilling partner," Zak replied in a low voice, dragging his eyes back to mine. I had to concede that he had a point.

"I need to go," I whispered. He studied me carefully, his fingers slowly inched up and I swallowed hard.

"Zak," Ronan called a warning again.

Zak closed his eyes and seemed to be trying to get a hold of himself. Slowly, he slid his hands back to my hips where he gripped me and set me back on my feet. I locked my knees, shocked to feel how unsteady I was.

"So, uh… I should probably be getting back now," I pointed out a little uncertainly. I didn't really want to go, but I felt like it was time to leave before I found myself in a position sober me wasn't prepared for.

"Already?" Ronan asked. I smiled softly but nodded.

"Yeah."

"I'll walk you back to your room," Zak offered, and he finished his breakfast.

"No, really, it's…" The words died on my lips at the look Zak gave me. Oookay.

"Don't be too long, we have inventory to do today," Ronan told Zak, and I flicked my gaze to him.

He stood leaning back against the other counter, his arms crossed over his chest, his dark eyes considering me carefully. Slowly, almost deliberately, he kept eye contact with me as he lowered one hand to his crotch. My eyes widened at the hard length I could see imprinted there as he adjusted himself.

Was he… Did watching us…

"Give me a sec to put on some clothes and grab my shoes," Zak told me softly.

Nodding, I slid away with my head down as I hurried for the door. I slipped on my shoes and was straightening up when I heard them speak again.

"Don't come on too strong, you scared her off," Ronan said quietly, as if he were trying to prevent me from hearing them.

"She liked me coming on strong. You saw the way she reacted. She's into it, she just doesn't know it," Zak replied.

I frowned. Into what?

"I know she is, fuck. Last night she… she took to it without pause. But in the light of day, she might not want this. Just don't push her. We can tell by now who has experience and who doesn't. She may as well be a virgin with how vanilla she is. Just… take it easy. No pressure, remember?" Ronan reminded.

"Yeah, yeah," Zak replied dismissively. I quickly turned my back to them and put my hand on the doorknob as if I had been just about to leave.

What the hell had they been talking about? And what did they mean I was vanilla? I wasn't a virgin, not in the least. But the way they spoke was as if I didn't know anything at all. And why the hell did it matter what they thought?

"Ready?"

I jumped, having not heard Zak step up beside me. For a large man, he really did move quietly.

"Yes," I answered and quickly flung open the door. I was out and headed for the stairs before he even left the flat.

"Hold up, what's the rush?" Zak called out.

"No rush, I just want to go home," I answered without turning back. Zak caught up in no time and I waited as he pulled keys from his pocket.

"Hazel," he said softly. It was the first time I could remember him saying my name, and it had a shiver of awareness running down my spine.

"I'm sorry if I made you uncomfortable this morning. I hope you know I'd never do anything to hurt you," he apologized.

"But I don't know that," I countered, finally lifting my eyes to meet his. "I don't know you."

He nodded slowly and raked a hand through his hair again. "You spent the morning talking to Ronan, and some of last night, so you know him a little better. Maybe we can take our time going back to your room and *we* can talk?" he offered.

I frowned. "What's the point? I'm going home anyway, and I don't understand why it matters to you," I returned, watching him carefully. He raised an eyebrow and his eyes skittered over me again, hesitating on my breasts briefly before meeting my gaze again.

"You can't think of a reason?" he asked. I glared, but it was ruined by my cheeks warming and the small smile that tugged at my lips. The man had an irresistible charm.

"Like I said, I'm going home," I reminded.

He shrugged. "Maybe, but that doesn't mean you have to leave now or even tonight. From what you told us last night, you could use the break and the... distraction."

I ducked my head, letting my hair fall forward to conceal my smile. He was a ruthless flirt. "What would we even talk about?" I asked, indicating to the door.

He grinned. "Well, let's start with the basics."

"Like favorite colors, foods, etcetera?"

"Sure, if you like. I was going to ask your favorite position in bed and when you lost your virginity, but sure, let's start with prep level questions."

A startled laugh escaped me, and I caught his smug grin as he opened the door. I stepped out, blinking at the sunlight and waited for him to close up behind me. The street looked different in the sunlight, and I could honestly say that I probably wouldn't have stopped here had I seen it like this. No, it wasn't filthy, but there was an almost creepy, abandoned feel to it in the light of day than there had been the night before.

"Everyone will be sleeping it off," Zak informed me as if he'd read my mind. "We're a small town, and this is the only bar around. There's not a lot else to do on the weekends."

I nodded and slowly started towards my room, purposely lagging behind. Zak had asked for time.

"Okay, I was nineteen when I lost my virginity to my fiancé, Richard. I haven't been with any other men. As for positions? Well... Rich likes to, uh..." I trailed off, feeling my cheeks warm and my stomach lurch. "Rich liked to take me from behind. I didn't mind it, but I liked him on top no matter what," I answered with a shrug.

"Were you able to get off when you were in doggy?" he asked. I sucked in a breath, trying not to be embarrassed by the topic we were discussing.

"That's kind of personal," I said instead.

He shrugged. "I'll take that as a no."

I frowned. He was right, but it was annoying.

"And you always liked him on top. Was it because you couldn't be bothered to do the work, or because you like not to be in control?" he continued. I hesitated, trying to force myself not to be so awkward.

"I like my partner to have control," I answered quickly without looking at him. "What about you?"

He smiled. "I was fifteen, she was seventeen and my father's boss's daughter. Christmas party," he explained. I gasped and he shook his head, grinning. "And I like all kinds of positions. The more adventurous, the better," he added. The way he said that had me frowning. I was sure he hadn't answered that as truthfully as he could have.

"I don't suppose I need to ask you if you ever had trouble getting off. You guys are lucky like that," I muttered.

"Three times," he admitted without hesitation. I stopped and turned to look at him in surprise. "I like a woman who isn't shy to tell me what she likes. I like it when I can hear how much pleasure I give her. I was with this woman once who was too quiet. I could *feel* that she got off, that she was enjoying it, but she didn't so much as make a peep. Then there was this woman who made *too much* noise. I'd barely kissed her, and she was moaning like I had my tongue between her legs. That was a huge turn-off," he explained.

"And the third time?" I asked, pushing past the graphic imagery his explanations put in my head.

"She didn't like to experiment. It was… okay, I guess. But it was missionary, and she was a big taker and not much of a giver. I got bored," he admitted. I blinked in surprise and shook my head.

"Wow… you're very open about all of this," I pointed out as we reached my door. I tugged the key free from my bag and opened the door, glad to see nothing inside had been moved.

"Only with people I'm hoping will need the information," he admitted. I couldn't fight my smile this time and stepped into the doorway of my room, turning to face him as I shook my head. "You're persistent."

"Yeah, well… When I see something I like, I go for it."

"I'm still getting over someone," I reminded softly.

He grinned and leaned in closer to me, brushing my hair back behind my ear.

"You know what they say about getting over someone," he reminded.

I rolled my eyes and scoffed. "Yeah, sure. To get under someone else."

Zak stepped in closer so that I had to tilt my head back to look at him.

"Or between two of us," he countered.

My gaze snapped from his lips to his face, and he watched me carefully. Did he mean... Ronan and him... together? An image flooded my mind, the three of us kneeling in that big bed upstairs in their flat, Zak kissing my lips, his hands on my breasts, sliding his shaft in and out of my pussy. And Ronan behind me, his fingers on my clit, his lips on my neck and his big, hard—woah.

"Uh," I mumbled, my mouth dry and my mind short-circuiting. Zak grinned as if he knew something I didn't. Then before I could mount any kind of protest, he swooped down and kissed me. I didn't even fight him, didn't resist. Part of it had to be shock from what he'd just suggested.

I kissed him back and he slid a hand to my lower back, pulling me against him so that I could feel his erection throbbing between us. The moan that broke free from me was startling, and I heard him groan low, his tongue slipping into my mouth. I broke away when air became necessary and he pressed his forehead against mine, refusing to let me go.

"Zak," I whispered, my hands on his chest

He pulled back enough to look down at my upturned face and brushed his thumb across my lower lip.

"Just think about it," he suggested, his dark eyes searching my face. "We'll be working tonight if you decide you want to be adventurous."

I swallowed hard, trying hard to find the right words when he stepped back.

"I hope to see you later, baby girl," he added and then he turned around and was gone.

CHAPTER SIX

I closed the door to my room and leaned my back against it, my
heart pounding, and my body oddly electrified. This had to be
the strangest morning of my life.

The opportunity to be with two men.

At once.

It was obvious from that earlier conversation I'd overheard
between Zak and Ronan how comfortable they were with one
another; that this was something they did often. Why would they
ask *me*? They thought I was *vanilla*... I guess that meant I was
boring in bed.

I had next to no experience. I wasn't even enough to keep my
fiancé interested. So why did these two drop-dead gorgeous men
want me in their bed? It had to be because I was new and shiny,
and they were bored with the local stock.

I shook my head to rid myself of the images in my mind of the
three of us in bed. Why did it matter? I was going home now...
wasn't I?

I glanced at my bed where my phone was and grimaced. It was
probably time for me to check my messages and let Momma and
Daddy know I was alive at least. Groaning, I pushed away from
the door and turned my phone on. I waited and sighed in dismay
at the number of missed calls, voicemails, and texts I had.

When the phone finally stopped vibrating, I scrolled straight to
my momma's number where several texts and missed call
notifications awaited me. I sent her a text first because I didn't
want to talk to her. She'd only worry and try to guilt me into
leaving.

But I *was* leaving... wasn't I?

I paused while typing out my message and frowned. Was I staying or was I going? I didn't want to go home right now; I didn't want to face what was waiting for me there and the questions I'd have to answer. And how would I even begin to explain it all? As furious as I was with my fiancé and my best friend, my stupid, soft heart just couldn't bring me to trash them like that.

I wasn't ready to go home. I wasn't ready to face my reality yet. That didn't mean I was going to stay and take up Zak's offer to sleep with him and his friend, but I definitely wasn't going home. I typed out a quick message to my momma, asked her to give Daddy a hug for me, and then I turned off my phone again. I was not in the mood to speak to anyone, and they would all want to know where I was. It may be cowardly, but I wasn't ready to face any of them yet, and the last thing I needed was for them to show up.

Blinking up at the ceiling, I pondered my options. What was I going to do? Right now, I needed to do something other than go over the same questions in my head. Pushing myself up off the bed, I looked over my clothing options again. I had a pair of yoga pants and a tank top. I snatched up the clothes and decided on going for a jog, and then I'd do yoga in my room to help keep me calm. After that, I'd grab some lunch and a shower and maybe another nap since I was still tired from last night. With a nod at myself, I removed the shirt and paused in putting it down. A smile tugged at my lips as I looked at Ronan's shirt and I tried not to blush at remembering this morning's events. I had certainly never been in that situation before, and I was monumentally grateful that it had been those two who had stuck with me throughout the night and kept me safe. It made me shiver to think about how stupid I'd been and how vulnerable I'd left myself. Neither of them had pushed me for more when they clearly could have

I swallowed, my breath hitching and body reacting as my mind drifted back to Zak's suggestion.

I shook my head hard and dropped the shirt. No, I wasn't that kind of girl. I mean, yes, I wanted to be adventurous and brave, but I didn't mean it like *that*. Last night was a total fluke in my behavior. Ronan was right. In comparison to what they had offered me, I was *very* vanilla.

I hung the shirt over the back of a chair and quickly changed for my run. I twisted my hair up into a messy ponytail, sorted through my scattered supplies for my sunglasses, and then hurriedly slipped on my runners.

~

Hours later, I had gone for a run, showered, eaten, and tormented myself with all of my questions of self-worth before finally passing out. I'd woken two hours ago, munched on an apple, then showered again for the sake of it. As I wandered around my room, I brushed and styled my hair because I wanted to feel pretty. *Not* because I was considering going over to the bar.

I wanted to look nice.

For me.

In this dingy hotel room.

Where no one would see me.

After lecturing myself on how bad a habit it was to lie to ones-self, I finally admitted that curiosity was getting the better of me. I couldn't just sit here all night and wonder. But could I go through with what the guys had clearly wanted?

I stared down at my clothing choices laid out on my bed and twisted my lips in indecision. I had the dress I'd worn last night which I'd since washed and dried, or I had jeans and a cute tank top. Considering the atmosphere at the bar, the jeans and top would be better suited. However, it would not give me the confidence boost I was going to need if I was going to go through with this.

Was I going to go through with this?

I had gone for my run, but the entire time, instead of stressing over the state of my relationship with my fiancé and my best friend, my mind had played this morning on a loop, going over every look, every touch, every word. Eventually, I'd gotten to the point where I was convinced I'd exaggerated everything. The only way to find out was to go back tonight and see.

But I knew going to the bar tonight would be me agreeing to this... this thing between us. I mean, I was pretty sure if I wanted to back out, they wouldn't push the issue. However, I didn't want to be *that* girl. If I went tonight, I was going to be adventurous and brave, I was going to have fun and be someone that *wasn't* me for a change. And Zak and Ronan? They may be strangers, but I'd never felt safer while so scantily clothed in all my life. Something about them told me I was safe... and in a *lot* of trouble.

But it was the kind of trouble I was looking for.

I snatched up the dress again and tugged it on. I opted out of wearing a bra tonight and stuck with a lace thong. Moving to the mirror, I refused to let myself think about where I was going or why, and simply put on a little makeup. I made my eyes smokier than normal, and my lipstick a little darker. I fluffed out my hair, adjusted the girls so that I had cleavage and stepped back to look at myself. My gray eyes stood out in contrast to my dark hair and pale face, but the smokey eyeshadow enhanced them perfectly. I was overdressed for the bar, but I felt beautiful and sexy. I hoped it would give me the courage to go through with this.

Two men... at the same time.

Doubt began to tug at me. There was no way I could have

misconstrued Zak's earlier statement, was there? And what if he was just teasing? No, Zak didn't seem the type to do that, not about this. What if I backed out? What if I disappointed them? Zak had said he hated boring and plain, but that was all I knew in comparison to what they seemed to like.

I bit my lower lip and felt self-doubt crowd close.

"No!" I snapped at myself and huffed. "You are going to walk out that door and across the road. You are going to look that sexy, God-like man in the face and tell him what you want. Then you're going to get some liquid courage before you pass out from nerves and then dance to distract yourself. You are going to live tonight as if you are someone else; as if you haven't a care in the world," I lectured.

Nodding to my reflection, I grabbed my small bag, tossed in my phone, makeup, spare panties, and room key, and strode out of the room without giving myself another chance to back out.

I was halfway across the road when I began to reconsider this decision. Other patrons were already drinking, spilled out across the porch and in the parking lot. The music was loud, and the general atmosphere was fun and noisy.

"Come on, Hazel. You are doing this," I ordered myself.

I ignored a few obvious leers and pushed open the saloon style doors, pausing to give my eyes a second to adjust to the dimmer lighting inside compared to the bright spotlights in the parking lot.

"Baby girl," a deep voice rumbled. A shiver of anticipation ran down my back and I turned slowly to see Zak standing behind me, a half-smile on his face, his dark eyes considering me.

"Zak," I greeted as I raised my voice to be heard over the noise, and still somehow, I managed to sound breathy. He stepped in close, and I sucked in a breath, getting a lungful of whatever cologne he was wearing. It made my head dizzy, and my body suddenly felt electrified.

"You stayed," Zak pointed out.

"I did," I answered, not stepping back even as he edged closer, closing the gap between us.

"And you came here."

Again, I nodded. His eyes searched my face for a moment and then he smiled slowly, heatedly, and I felt my knees shake.

"Go get a drink, baby girl. Tonight, Ronan and I are looking after you," he told me, sliding his thumb over my cheek. My body warmed, but I couldn't move or speak. His thumb brushed over my lower lip, and I instinctively flicked my tongue out. His dark eyes seemed to darken more, and I could have sworn he groaned.

"Go get a drink, baby," he ordered, pulling back with obvious reluctance.

With one last look, I nodded and turned towards the bar. I could already feel Ronan's gaze on me, and when I lifted my eyes to look, I almost stumbled. God damn, these men were freaking gorgeous.

"Hello, sweetheart," he greeted, leaning closer to the bar as I took a vacant stool.

"Hi, Ronan," I acknowledged, trying not to sound shy. I was meant to be sure, confident, and sexy, not timid, and out of my depth. Which I was... but that wasn't the point.

"How do you feel?" he asked, his gaze sweeping over me carefully.

"Better. I slept, I drank water, and I ate," I answered, feeling my shoulders loosen.

"Good, I'm glad. What will it be tonight?" he asked.

"Another fireball?"

He grinned. "Coming right up."

As soon as he placed the shot glass on the bar, I scooped it up and downed it, scrunching up my eyes at the burn.

"Another?"

Ronan nodded slowly and poured me one, but before I could take it, he leaned in close.

"Zak and I won't touch a drunk woman. Do you understand?" he asked, his gaze dark and intense.

"Last night in your office—"

"Shouldn't have happened," he interrupted. "I don't regret it; it was fucking amazing. But generally, if a woman has been drinking, we won't go there."

Butterflies let loose in my stomach, and I took a shaky breath before I nodded.

"I understand," I finally answered. Ronan let go of the shot glass and I downed it before pushing it away. He placed a bottle of water on the bar, and I frowned.

"Hydrate," he ordered.

"I'm good," I answered. Ronan didn't move, didn't speak, and yet somehow, he was... more. There was an air to him that told me he didn't like to repeat himself. It crackled with some unknown force, but I felt that it was in my best interest to listen.

"Drink," he ordered again, softer this time, but there was a calmness there that gave me pause.

"And if I don't?" I asked, wanting to test the waters when I disobeyed a minor command.

He shrugged. "I want to look after you. I mean that in more ways than one. I won't touch you if you're drunk or even tipsy. You need water... if you've decided to go through with our plans for tonight."

My chest tightened and I cleared my throat.

Without another word, I took the bottle and opened it. Zak watched as I took a few mouthfuls before putting the cap back on. He nodded approvingly before he winked and made his way down the bar.

Wow.

Where Zak was pure energy and lust, good-times, easy-times, and pleasure—Ronan was something else. He was still gorgeous, and he still made me feel safe, but there was an edge to him that warned me not to cross him. I don't know how I knew. He'd never done or said anything that made me think he would get physical if I refused to listen to him, but there was a commanding presence in the set of his shoulders, in the glittering darkness of his eyes, and the shape of his lips.

Ronan was most definitely a man who needed to be in charge. I took another sip of water before I tucked it under a lip on the other side of the bar. Ronan watched me and I waved, and weaved my way between people as I made my way to the dance floor. I needed to move; I needed to do something to work off this nervous energy and to distract myself from my decision. Because no matter what, I was going through with this tonight.

Out on the dance floor I swayed to the music and closed my eyes, losing myself in it. Raising my arms, I danced with other people, not caring who they were or how long we danced, I just let myself get lost. I forgot all about my life, the people in it and what was expected of me, and I ignored the memories of my fiancé and best friend.

I just danced.

Closing my eyes to lose myself in the beat, I danced with strangers, but never too closely or too long. I drank more water and had another shot, but when my head began to spin a little, I stopped the alcohol. I wanted to be someone else tonight, I wanted to try something new, something hot, something *not me*. And if Ronan was telling the truth when he said he wouldn't touch me if I was so much as tipsy, then I needed to cut back. When I went to the bar a third time, Ronan met me with a shot. I shook my head and asked for water instead. He leaned in close as he placed the bottle on the bar and indicated with a crook of his finger for me to lean in. I did as he asked, and his thumb brushed over my cheek, and his lips just barely touched mine. I sucked in a surprised breath, and he pulled back, heated chocolate eyes locked on mine.

"Good girl," he whispered before he stepped away and got back to work.

I swallowed hard and sat back, my heart thudding and my skin prickling. The heated look he gave me combined with that barest brush of his lips had me squirming in my seat. It was insane how much his praise for me asking for the responsible drink made me want to cheer. What the hell was this man doing to me?

After downing a quarter of the bottle, I slipped it in my place under the bar lip and went back to the dance floor. I passed Zak on the way, and he smirked at me. His grin was so infectious I couldn't help but smile back.

Between the music and the dancing, I lost track of time, of how long I was out there letting the world fade until there was nothing but the beat of the music and the sway of my hips. Hands slid around my waist, and I leaned back against a hard, steady body. The prickling of my skin told me that this wasn't just some random person touching me. I didn't fight it as his hands slid up my waist, along my bare arms to move my hair over one shoulder. Lips brushed the skin there and I shivered, already knowing it was Zak who held me, whose body was pressed firmly against mine. It was Zak's hands gently gripping my upper arms and whose lips were moving along my shoulder to my neck to nip it lightly.

Another set of hands slid around my hips, pressed close to my front, and I opened my eyes to see Ronan there. His dark eyes heated and glittered with something else, something forbidden.

My heart kicked up another notch and he danced closer so that I was sandwiched between the two strong men.

None of us spoke, we simply swayed together, feeling each other move. Zak slowly turned me around and Ronan's arms wrapped around me as Zak leaned in close. For another song we danced like this. I didn't even bother to look at everyone around us who must have some thoughts about how the three of us were dancing. For the first time ever, I didn't care what other people were thinking; their judgements meant nothing to me. The only thing that mattered right now was these two men and the way they were making me feel.

Zak glanced over my shoulder to Ronan and nodded slightly before he leaned in to gently kiss my cheek, and then he turned around and left.

"Are you ready?" Ronan asked. I tracked Zak with my eyes and watched as he opened a door to a stairway before he turned back to look at us.

Was I ready? I refused to give myself time to think about it and nodded.

Ronan stepped around to my front, searching my face intently. I wasn't sure what he was looking for, but he must have found it because he tangled his fingers with mine and tugged me forward. My knees felt a little weak, but I followed behind Ronan as he led me towards his apartment stairs.

CHAPTER SEVEN

Zak closed the door to the apartment behind us, and the lock sounded unnaturally loud in the near silence of the room, only the faded sounds of music penetrated the walls.

"Who is minding the bar if you guys are up here?" I asked nervously.

"We have a manager and other bar staff," Zak answered. "Would you like a drink?"

I nodded, not trusting my voice. I wanted to be confident. I wanted to be sexy and sure of myself, and if I spoke, they would know I was anything but.

"Why don't you take a seat, and get comfortable," Ronan suggested before he squeezed my hand and entered the kitchen with Zak, leaving me alone.

With my heart pounding and my mouth dry, I moved slowly towards the lounge. It looked ridiculously comfortable, and I kicked off my shoes and placed my bag down on the small end table. I didn't sit though, too nervous to sit still and wait.

Instead, I moved towards the bookshelf and read the titles on the spines. There were a lot of non-fiction books about the world, philosophy, and law. I kept browsing, smiling when I saw a few fiction books, but of course, they were thrillers and action based. Moving along, I paused at some female romance author names. I didn't recognize the names, but judging by the book titles, they were *definitely* sexy books.

Seven Rue, Quell T. Fox, Leeah Taylor, Sara Cate, and Katee Robert.
Did the guys enjoy these books, or did they serve another purpose? Were they perhaps left here by an ex-girlfriend?

The bottom shelf held books about music, and it was then I noted the guitar in the corner, and I wondered which one of them played. I was about to straighten up when my gaze caught on a handful of books towards the end.

BDSM and Kinks in the Bedroom. Bondage and Babes. Doms, Subs, and BDSM.

"Here," Ronan said as he stepped up beside me suddenly.

I jumped, feeling heat leech into my face at being caught. I felt as though I'd just been caught reading his journal. But I shouldn't feel guilty; the books were right there for anyone to read.

Was that what I was in for tonight?

I turned as Ronan handed me a glass and I smiled as I took it. Watching him, I took a healthy swig, noting the way his dark eyes followed the drink to my lips where they lingered. I lowered the glass, and without looking away from my face, he took the glass and placed it on the bookshelf before stepping in close.

Butterflies let loose in my stomach, and I smiled nervously as he slowly raised his hand and used a gentle finger to tip my head back.

"You look beautiful tonight, sweetheart," Ronan said softly.

"Thank you."

My reply was soft, barely audible, and I tried to steady myself, tried to pull myself together. God, I was so out of my depth here. I was going to disappoint them; I was going to let them down!

Slowly, I assume so that I had time to back out if I wanted to, Ronan leaned in towards me. But I didn't pull away. I parted my lips in anticipation, and my eyes fell closed as his soft lips brushed mine, once, twice, before he pressed harder, kissing me more intently.

Oh, lordy.

I sank against him, kissing him back, and he growled low. A thrill shot up my spine at that sound, and his tongue slipped between my lips, kissing me deeper, his hands on my hips pulling me closer. I slid my shaky hands up his arms to bunch in his shirt near his collar as I immersed myself in his kiss, in the feel of his hard body pressed against mine.

God, the man could kiss; there was no hurry, no intense escalation of passion. He was kissing me like he was exploring, like we had all the time in the world. Why hadn't I ever been kissed like this before? Like I was worth exploring.

On and on the kiss went, and my breath was coming shorter, heavier, my body alive and sensitive. Sometime later, Ronan began moving me backwards, small, slow steps so that we were almost swaying, dancing. I was so wrapped up in him that I didn't notice we'd made it to the couch until he turned us around on the spot. He pulled away and sat back on the couch and I was almost panting, trying to get my breath back.

Ronan looked up at me with dark, hooded eyes, his lips slightly swollen. He was breathing heavier now too, something that made me strangely satisfied that this man, so used to being in control, was reacting like this to me simply kissing him. He tangled his fingers with mine and tugged gently, his gaze never wavering from my face.

"Come here," he ordered softly. I stumbled forward and leaned over him. Ronan smirked and gripped my waist, pulling me down onto his lap. I bit back a gasp and found myself straddling his lap, my dress pushing up and barely covering my thong.

"Kiss me," he ordered again. I smiled and did as he asked, having no problem kissing him again and again. He was addictive, different. Including Ronan and Zak, I'd kissed only five men in my life and slept with one. Every way Ronan and Zak touched me was different, but it was exciting, and I wanted more.

Settling over him more comfortably, I leaned forward until I was better aligned on his lap and kissed him again. He didn't kiss me slowly this time, he took from me what he wanted, and I let him. I pressed my lips against his, attempting to do so with the same fervor and intensity he showed me. His hands were on my knees and slowly sliding up my thighs, leaving a fiery trail everywhere he touched. I slid my hands to the hem of his shirt and carefully edged them beneath it. My fingers connected with his skin, and he stiffened for a moment but didn't pull away. Up and up my hands slid, feeling the hard ridges of his body, and the thin layer of chest hair. Ronan's grip on my hips tightened and he pulled me down against him, harder, grinding his hips upwards. I moaned against him as a zap of pleasure spun through me.

Another pair of hands slid up the side of my waist and I jolted away from Ronan's lips. He was looking up at me with a studying expression, waiting. I realized that Ronan's hands were still on my hips, but another pair were running up and down my waist, brushing the sides of my breasts and then back down.

Zak.

I'd all but forgotten he was here too with how involved I was with kissing Ronan.

"He's just touching you, sweetheart. But if at any moment you want to stop, say vanilla," Ronan murmured.

"Vanilla?" I repeated, slightly breathless. "Why not ask you to stop?"

He ground his hips upwards again and I gasped, clinging to his shirt. "We don't want to scare you away," he replied after a small hesitation, sharing a knowing look with Zak.

I shook my head. "I need to know."

Zak's hands were still sliding up and down my waist, sometimes sliding around to my front to touch my stomach, his fingers grazing the underside of my breasts but never going too far.

"Because, baby girl, sometimes when someone says stop in the way we do things, they don't actually mean it. And the word "stop" can be a turn-on," Zak answered in my ear, his deep voice a rumble of sound that sent a shiver of awareness down my spine. Oh.

"We won't do anything you don't want to do. We like to push boundaries, we like to try new things, and we want to teach you some things, let you experience how pleasure can come in many forms," Zak continued, running his lips along my shoulder to my neck. I closed my eyes and tipped my head to the side to give him greater access, feeling Ronan rock beneath me again.

"And if I say the word, you'll stop? No matter what we're doing, no matter how much you're enjoying it?" I asked softly, a small sense of doubt niggling at my mind. Zak's hands disappeared from me, and I opened my eyes when Ronan tilted my head back up. I blinked at seeing them both sitting beside one another, their faces oddly serious.

"There is no pleasure for us in an unwilling partner. There is no pleasure in causing a woman harm, and there is no desire in either of us to become monsters. What we do may be unconventional to most people, but we want to enjoy your body, and we want you to enjoy the experience as well, probably more so," Ronan told me, holding my gaze the entire time.

"Call it a point of pride, if you will, but no woman in our care will ever go without feeling safe and thoroughly pleasured," Zak added.

Heat spread up my neck to my cheeks. It was silly, I know. I knew why I was there; I knew what I was agreeing to. But the thought of these two incredibly drool-worthy men lavishing that much attention on me was a heady sensation.

"Hazel." Ronan said my name seriously, intensely. "Whether we're just touching you, kissing you, or if one or both of us are inside you... if you use that word, we stop. End of story."

I nodded, a part of my mind easing at his words. He sounded

serious, and I felt as though he was being honest.

"We want to take care of you, Hazel. We want you to experience intense pleasure, but to do that, we need you to trust us. There might be times you feel uncomfortable or worried. We need you to believe us when we say nothing is more important than your safety and satisfaction. We will never harm you. Everything we do is meant to bring you pleasure beyond your knowledge. Can you do that? Can you trust us?" Zak asked.

I hesitated as I thought about it. Neither of them was touching me now. Zak was sitting on the couch and Ronan's hands were by his side. There was no manipulation, they were both stating the facts and asking me to accept them. Did I trust them? Did I trust myself? If this turned out to be a huge mistake, could I accept it? A flash of my fiancé with my best friend raced in my mind and I shut it down.

"I want to feel," I whispered.

"Do you trust us?" Zak pushed, unrelenting, his brown eyes deadly serious. Ronan was watching me with that same steady look, searching, watching me for even the hint of a lie. But I wanted this, and for whatever reason, I felt like I could trust these two to stop if I asked, and to give me what I needed.

"I trust you; both of you," I answered, making sure to look at each of them. Ronan nodded his approval, and my gaze flicked between both men and their obvious erections. Self-doubt stabbed at me, and I ducked my head.

"What is it?" Ronan urged, frowning. I flicked a glance at him and found it strange that this man could read me so well so quickly.

"It's nothing."

"Hazel."

That's all he said, my name. But the tone he used, that whip of command in his voice, had me almost falling over myself to answer him.

"I, uh… I'm fine," I assured.

"Baby girl… this is outside your normal," Zak started softly. "We need you to be open with us, we need to be able to talk about everything, even the awkward things—especially the awkward things. Nothing you say will make us want you any less. But to make this an enjoyable experience for you, we need to know when something is on your mind."

My mortification grew and I gnawed on my lower lip while I tried to find the words. "I… I'm worried," I whispered, looking away from them.

"That we'll hurt you? That we won't stop if you ask us to?" Ronan questioned.

I shook my head. "No, I trust you there. I'm worried that… that I'm going to disappoint you," I said in a rush, keeping my eyes glued to the little bit of ink I could see peeking out from beneath Ronan's shirt near his collar bone. I knew he had one arm inked down to his elbow, but I wasn't sure if his tattoos were as extensive as Zak's.

"Hazel, look at me," Ronan commanded. I refused, too embarrassed. I wanted to crawl off his lap. God, this was so humiliating. Here I was, trying to be the confident seductress, but when we actually got down to things, I was letting my insecurities get the better of me.

"Sweetheart," he tried again, tugging at my hair, and the gentle, playful gesture sent warmth spreading across my chest. Slowly, I dragged my gaze upwards to see them both looking at me with a mixture of incredulity and sadness.

"Who made you feel that way? Your fiancé?" Ronan asked.

"I… I guess."

"No, I think it started earlier," Zak commented, searching my face carefully. "My guess is your parents. From what you told us last night, they made their expectations of you pretty clear. And your fiancé cheating on you on top of it only solidified your perceived low worth."

I blinked in surprise. "Are you a therapist?"

He smirked and shook his head. "No, but it pays to be able to read people when the sex you like is unconventional," Zak answered.

"So, you don't feel like you're enough for us? You're worried we won't enjoy ourselves?" Ronan interrupted. I nodded, trying to get a read on him.

There was a small pause before Zak leaned forward to kiss me hard. He didn't explore like Ronan did, he didn't ease me into it. He plundered, he took, he demanded. I made a sound of surprise and kissed him back, enjoying the differences in the way they both kissed, but I was unable to decide which I liked best.

Zak pulled away and grinned at me, and before I could catch my breath, Ronan was there, his lips commanding mine, his hands in my hair tugging, angling me the way he needed. When he pulled away, I gaped at them both, shocked.

"I guess it's up to us to make you realize just how goddamn perfect you are," Ronan whispered roughly.

I didn't say anything to that, but I don't think either of them expected me to. Zak slid off the couch and I watched as he pulled over a small, cushioned stool. It was wide and set low and I frowned as he dragged it to the floor behind me and knelt on it. I was going to ask what he was doing, but Ronan gripped my chin lightly in his fingers and turned my gaze back to his. Without giving me time to speak, he claimed my mouth once again, his hands sliding back up my thighs, inching higher.

Zak's hands slid around my waist once more, running up the length of me before sliding around my front. Again and again, he ran his hands over me, sliding up my back, across my arms, around to my stomach before he'd repeat the process again. I found myself relaxing into Ronan, his mouth leisurely exploring mine, his hands sliding up and down my thighs, edging ever closer to my throbbing center before sliding back down to my knees. Each drag of his hands brought him nearer to my core again but never quite touching me where I needed him.

It caught me off guard when Zak's hands slid to the zipper at the back of my dress and slowly slid it down. I pulled back slightly, but Ronan's hand was at the back of my head in an instant, bunching in my hair, refusing to allow me to move away more than an inch from his face.

"Easy, sweetheart. Eyes on me. Just kiss me," he whispered thickly, breathlessly.

My breath was choppy as I nodded and leaned forward to kiss Ronan again as Zak slid the zipper of my dress all the way down. He was gentle as he slid the straps down my arms until the dress was bunched at my hips.

I swallowed and nodded, kissing Ronan again as I felt Zak slide the zipper all the way down before he gently slipped the straps down my arms until my dress was bunched down at my hips. The cool air on my skin was noticeable, and I shivered when warm skin pressed against my back. Zak had obviously taken off his shirt at some point. I wanted to turn around and look at him, to feel him, but Ronan's hand in my hair kept my head pulled down towards his. Zak continued to run his hands across my skin, my back, my stomach, my waist, repeating that same process he'd done before, but this time I was able to feel the slightly calloused fingers on sensitive skin, causing me to shiver. Ronan ground up against me, and I moaned against his lips, getting dizzy but unwilling to stop kissing him. I *needed* to kiss him, not just because of how I felt when doing it, but because if I gave myself too much time to think about the fact that I had two sets of hands on me at once, and that I was here to be with two men at the same time, then I would probably wuss out. And I wanted to try this, to experience it.

I wanted to be reckless and adventurous.

I was tired of being the good girl.

CHAPTER EIGHT

Zak's hands slid from my stomach and moved upwards, this time cupping my breasts. I arched into his hands, hoping to feel some relief from the constant teasing these two were doing. Both were touching me, but up until this point, neither of them had *touched me*. Ronan let me pull away long enough to breathe, to pant, to arch against Zak's exploring hands again. The whole time, Ronan's gaze never left my face. My skin rippled with goosebumps, and I was suddenly very aware that I was straddling one man, almost naked, while the second brought his large hands up to cup my breasts. There was the constant, aching throb between my legs; my skin oversensitive and aware of every movement and stroke.

Closing my eyes, I moaned as Zak's fingers feathered over my nipples. He tugged and rolled and squeezed, and I rocked against Ronan's hard length that was trapped in his jeans. I slid my fingers down his shirt and began to tug at the button there, but Ronan stopped me with a hand over mine. I blinked at him, and he shook his head.

"Aren't you uncomfortable?"

"I want to watch you. This isn't about me right now," he replied roughly. I rocked again and I watched his jaw clench, but he didn't let me help him.

"Shuffle up a little more, baby girl," Zak whispered against my neck. I watched Ronan, waiting for him to release his hold on my hair and let me move.

"Good girl," he breathed when I waited for permission, and then he slowly let me go. A thrill went through me when he called me that, and I carefully edged further up his body. Zak pulled my hips back slightly as Ronan widened his knees, causing my legs to spread further apart and my ass to poke out. In a quick movement I hadn't even been able to follow, Zak pulled my dress all the way off and I was left in nothing but my lacey thong. I tried to move, but once again, Zak held my hips in place and Ronan's fingers were tangled in my hair.

"Eyes here, sweetheart," he reminded me.

"Fuck, you're gorgeous," Zak moaned behind me, his hands sliding over my bare ass cheeks. Heat washed over me again, and I was sure I was blushing.

Ronan's gaze zapped across my face, and there was a small smirk on his lips. "Kiss me."

I hesitated, and his grip on my hair tightened ever so slightly in warning. I gasped, but I was more shocked that I liked the small sting his grip caused. He must have seen it, known it, because his smirk widened and he pulled me down, crushing his lips to mine. I whimpered into his mouth, and Zak's hands resumed their exploration of my mostly naked body.

I wanted to grind down on Ronan, to find some relief, and yes, maybe tease the man beneath me who seemed to be so in control, but the way Zak had me kneeling left me bereft of anything to grind against.

As if he knew my need, Zak's hand slid from my belly down between my legs. I inhaled sharply, but Ronan refused to let me pull my lips away. His tongue plundered my mouth as Zak gently stroked me.

"Your pussy is soaked, baby girl," Zak groaned. I blushed harder knowing he was right, but no one had ever spoken to me like that before; no one had ever been so blunt or crude in their language. I loved it.

I moaned, louder this time, when Zak's hand slid beneath the thin scrap of lace to touch bare flesh. He teased my slit, running up and down the length of me, never letting me press harder into him. I whimpered; I was aching. I needed to feel him.

Zak's lips swept across my back and up to my neck again, even as Ronan continued to kiss me, torturing me with his tongue in my mouth and his hand in my hair.

"Do you want some relief, baby?" Zak whispered in my ear.

"Yes," I begged, panting as Ronan pulled away long enough for me to answer. My whole body was overheated, over-stimulated, needy, aching, and trembling.

"Yes, what?" Zak asked, sliding his finger gently over my clit. I moaned and bit my lower lip. Ronan's gaze followed that movement, entranced.

"Please?" I begged.

"You can call him master or sire," Ronan instructed. I paused, looking down at his face to see if I heard that correctly.

"Sire or master?" I repeated.

"Yes."

"And if I don't?" I asked, teasing, somewhat turned on by the thought of calling him sir and Zak sire.

What the hell was wrong with me?

Ronan's eyes narrowed and his grip on my hair tightened, the bite of pain somehow pleasurable. He gripped my thigh with one hand tightly and I gasped when a hot slap was struck against my backside. I jumped, and Zak brushed his thumb over the sting he'd just caused, easing it.

"Want to keep testing me?" Ronan asked. Another thrill shot through me at his words. Ronan definitely liked to call the shots; he was dominant and assertive, and he had to have his way. It was so strange that I found myself trembling with desire with that knowledge. It was strange that wanting to please him had become somewhat of a priority to me. Zak seemed to know Ronan well enough to know he needed this and what he wanted to happen and made it so.

Richard had never been into games or roleplay or anything. Our sex life had always been very, well… vanilla. And sparse, but that made more sense now, knowing he'd been getting some on the side. I banished those thoughts and stared down at Ronan who was still waiting.

"Hazel," he prompted, his jaw tight, and shoulders still.

"I understand… sir," I answered. He made a growling noise in his chest before he ravaged my lips again—hard, desperate, dominating. I let him take me, let him have control and take what he needed from me.

I shuddered against him as Zak slid a finger down my slit and then inside me. I tried to push back against his hand, but the angle I was kneeling at with Ronan's hand in my hair left me very little control. Ronan let me pull back as Zak pumped his finger into me again and again. I cried out, throwing my head back.

"You're drenched, baby," Zak moaned and then added a second finger. I moaned low, so on edge I was almost ready to topple over. "You're clenching my fingers so hard. You're almost there."

I tried to push back, to take his fingers harder, deeper, but Ronan's grip on my hips kept me exactly where I was. His gaze was on my face… intense, heated, excited.

"Come for him, sweetheart," Ronan encouraged gruffly.

"Oh, God,"

"Not God," he murmured. I moaned as Zak gently inserted a third finger. I winced slightly and he slowed down, careful, taking his time to help me adjust. It didn't take long and then I was struggling to grind against him again.

"Hazel," Ronan snapped in a hard voice. I blinked down at him, my focus straying as I climbed higher and higher.

"Come on his fingers," Ronan repeated. I closed my eyes and then gasped, my eyes flying open as Ronan bunched his fingers in my hair and tugged hard.

"Hazel," he growled.

"Yes! Yes, sir!" I screamed, throwing my head back as I clenched hard around Zak's thrusting fingers. I swear it was two orgasms, one right after the other, both causing me to clench around him tightly, my body shaking hard.

"That's it, baby," Zak murmured behind me with approval as he pumped his fingers inside me one last time before he slid them from my body. I panted, shook, my body still experiencing small waves of pleasure.

"Beautiful," Ronan whispered almost reverently as he tipped my face up to kiss me. I was surprised at how gentle he was considering how rough he'd been only moments ago, and I found myself sinking into it, still struggling to breathe evenly but loving the way he kissed me, the way his hands trailed up my stomach to cup my sensitive breasts.

There was a crinkling behind me, and I glanced down as an empty condom wrapper was thrown onto the couch beside me, and I realized Zak had done that on purpose to show me he'd covered up.

I glanced down, wondering if I'd see him, remembering how intimidating he'd looked this morning in his boxers; how big and hard he'd felt when he'd rocked himself against me on the kitchen counter, but Ronan tipped my face back up to him instead.

"Eyes on me, sweetheart. I want to watch your face when he slides his cock into you."

Holy. Shit.

I almost came again with those words.

Zak's lips were on my neck again, and I shivered when he grazed his teeth along the sensitive skin.

"Are you ready, baby girl?"

Zak's voice was deep and rough behind me, like he was on edge. I desperately wanted to see him, but Ronan was watching me. He wasn't controlling me right now, his hands were not in my hair, but he'd given me an order and I felt like he was giving me a chance to prove that I'd follow them.

"Yes, sire," I answered.

Ronan's eyes glittered and that devastating smirk tugged at his lips. Zak groaned behind me, and I stiffened a little at feeling him press against me.

"Relax, baby. You remember the word, yes? You say it, and we stop. No matter what, we want you to feel safe," he promised. My worry eased with his words. How the hell did these two practical strangers manage to make me feel so safe when I was in such a vulnerable position.

"Please, sire," I pleaded, turning my face to look at him over my shoulder. Zak kissed me hard, passionately, and then he pulled away. I made sure to bring my gaze back to Ronan who watched me with satisfaction.

"That's my girl," he praised. Something deep down inside me warmed at his words; a pleasure in satisfying this powerful man with a simple action. It was empowering, addictive. If I wasn't careful, I'd do anything to have him praise me, to make him happy.

I felt Zak then, the thick head of his shaft slowly sliding inside me. My mouth fell open, and I struggled to keep my gaze on Ronan when all I wanted to do was close my eyes and feel.

"Yes... relax, baby. You're drenched, but you're still so tight," Zak groaned, carefully sliding deeper inside me. Ronan slowly pushed me down, pressing me onto Zak's hard cock and I cried out, not expecting the movement. Zak groaned and his grip on my hips tightened as he began to thrust, pulling all the way out just to shove himself back inside me. My body resisted his intrusion, and I focused on relaxing, on letting him in. He was bigger than I'd thought—bigger than Rich was.

Ronan leaned forward and dipped his head to my chest where he flicked my nipple with his tongue.

"Yes," I moaned. He did the same to the other before he replaced his tongue with his fingers.

"Zak?" Ronan asked.

"Almost all the way in," Zak replied roughly, as if he were gritting his teeth.

"Relax for him, sweetheart. He isn't a small man. I warned you," Ronan ordered, stroking my breasts, watching my face intensely. *You'd know if Zak or I had fucked you.*

I remembered those words from this morning, and I nodded.

Yes, I was definitely going to be feeling this tomorrow morning.

Zak thrust upwards again, sharply, and I winced at the biting sting.

"Are you okay?" Ronan asked, stroking my cheek. I nodded and smiled softly.

"I'm in," Zak panted, his whole body practically vibrating behind me as if he were restraining himself.

"How do you feel, Hazel?" Ronan asked. I wasn't sure if I could blush anymore, but I was sure my face heated further.

"Full, amazing, *so good*."

Ronan smiled and leaned forward to kiss me and then Zak started moving. I moaned, pushing back gently as he thrust up. Ronan didn't stop me this time, and so I did it again. One of Zak's hands slid around to my front and began rubbing my clit as he drove in and out of me, picking up the pace and depth. I was lost in a sea of pleasure, unable to concentrate on anything. There was something decidedly wicked about being fucked by someone while on the lap of a man who was still fully clothed, his eyes intent on my face as I was driven closer and closer to heaven by another man's cock.

"You're getting closer, Hazel. I can feel it," Zak grunted, sheathing himself inside me over and over again. I don't know how long we did this, or how much time passed; I was too far gone, too overwhelmed with everything to know anything more than the pleasure that threatened to spill over with every thrust of his cock.

"You're doing so good, sweetheart, letting Zak fuck you like that. Do you know how good you're making him feel?" Ronan praised, stroking my breasts. I shuddered at his words, a wave of pleasure washing over me that had nothing to do with what Zak was doing. I felt... wanted. Here, between these two men, I felt *desired*.

"Ronan," Zak moaned, and his hand left my clit to run over my nipples. "Taste her."

I spasmed around Zak, almost coming at the deeply erotic sight of his fingers wiping my wetness on my breasts and Ronan lowering his mouth to them to taste me.

Ronan practically growled as he suckled hard on my breast, his tongue lashing out to lap up every tiny bit. "Delicious."

His dark eyes met mine as he licked his lips and I watched him lower his head to my other breast while Zak's fingers circled my clit again, his hard cock swelling.

"You're so fucking beautiful, Hazel. I could watch you take his cock all night long," Ronan admitted, his face an expression of ferocious need.

And suddenly I was screaming.

The orgasm ripped through me mercilessly. I threw my head back against Zak's shoulder as he pounded into me from behind. I heard the dull roar of his voice through my suddenly deaf ears as he found his own release, shaking and shuddering behind me, still thrusting as my inner muscles clamped hard around him. Ronan's teeth bit down lightly on my breast, and I cried out again, pleasure and plain mixing together as he suckled strongly, the pain subsiding.

I collapsed against Ronan's chest, my body wrung out and exhausted. Zak was rocking gently behind me, and I was still rippling around him, my body on a high unlike any other. Ronan kissed my cheek, his hands running up and down my arms. Zak's hands were stroking my back, his mouth pressing kisses along my shoulder and upper back.

"Are you okay?" Zak asked sometime later. I moaned slightly in response, exhausted. "Hazel? I need to know you're okay."

Slowly, I lifted my head and smiled, feeling drunk on the orgasm of a century.

"I'm more than okay, Zak," I whispered, figuring it was okay to call him by his name now as we were kind of done. Ronan searched my face and when he could see no sign of deceit, he grinned and kissed me, long and drugging. Zak slowly pulled out of me, and I winced slightly.

"You sure you're okay?"

"I am. I might be a little sore later. Zak is a lot bigger than my ex," I replied. Zak fell tiredly onto the couch beside us, a cocky grin on his face. I slid my gaze over him, noting that the condom had been disposed of and my eyes widened at his size. Oh... my... God. *That* had fit inside me? The man wasn't even fully erect anymore, and he was still massive.

Ronan, obviously reading the shock on my face, chuckled.

"That is part of the reason I did not want you to look at him when he took you," Ronan explained. I shook my head, grinning, and then I frowned when I fully registered what he'd said.

"What was the other reason?"

Ronan searched my face for a moment and smiled. "I wanted to watch your face. I think you've caught on already that I like to be in charge, and I like to be obeyed. Zak and I have done this together enough for us to know what each other needs and when."

"But you didn't... you haven't..." I stumbled over the words, still feeling how hard he was beneath me.

Ronan grinned and brushed a quick kiss over my lips. "This is new to you. I wanted to see how you went with the two of us here first. How you reacted to two of us touching you, kissing you, exploring you. I didn't want to do something you were not ready for. But the night is young, and if you're still happy to keep trying new things, I want to know what it feels like to have your pussy clamping around *my* cock when you come."

I gaped, my cheeks flooding with heat before I lowered my gaze, embarrassed. Ronan chuckled, and I looked back up at him when he cupped my face.

"After what we three just did, you're still embarrassed by the way I talk to you?"

I shrugged. "I'm not used to anyone speaking to me like that."

He tipped his head to the side in consideration and smiled.

"But you like it, don't you?" he asked softly. "You like hearing that you're being a good girl. I see it in your face every time I say it," he continued. I swallowed hard and nodded.

"And you like hearing us speak to you, telling you how hot your body is, how it feels to fuck you, to taste you," Zak added.

I turned to look at him and again and nodded. "I... I'm not sure what that says about me, but I like it."

"It makes you fucking hot," Zak replied.

I laughed and Ronan shrugged. "He's not wrong. But it also means you're meant for more than the vanilla lifestyle you've been living. And if you'll let us, we want to show you how much more there is to enjoy."

More.

There was more. I mean, I knew there was more, I wasn't a total prude; I read books, I watched TV, and I knew that Rich and I had led a plain sex-life. But holy heck, if things got any better than what I had just experienced, I wasn't sure I could handle it.

"You think about it. But first, I'm going to run you a bath. You stay here with Zak," Ronan said as he simply picked me up and put me on the other man's lap.

I smiled and Zak's arms wrapped around me.

CHAPTER NINE

"I didn't hurt you, did I? You were tighter than I thought, even after coming once," Zak asked.

I tried to suppress the heat in my cheeks, but judging from the grin Zak had, I hadn't been successful. Ronan came back with two water bottles before he left us alone again.

"Hazel?" Zak prompted. His eyes were full of concern as he waited, and I wanted to melt a little at how worried he was. It was strange how dominating and dirty-mouthed he could be during sex, but how concerned, gentle, and sweet he was afterwards.

I found I liked the differences.

"I'm fine, really. All I need is a little soak to get me back to normal," I assured.

After a moment he nodded and smiled warmly. I watched his perfect lips and leaned forward, pausing for a moment to see if he was okay with this. Zak's smile melted into a grin, and he brought me the rest of the way forward, pressing his lips against mine, exploring, and nipping. Zak kissed differently from Ronan, but it was no less enjoyable. I couldn't seem to get enough of either man; I was quickly becoming addicted. I never wanted to stop, but eventually we both had to breathe. We pulled apart, and I breathlessly accepted the water bottle Zak offered me again. I laughed lightly and took it, watching as he unscrewed his and took several mouthfuls. There was something sexy about watching the way his throat worked as he drank.

"Hazel?"

"Mmm?"

"Drink your water."

"Maybe later," I answered, distracted.

Zak's expression darkened and I hesitated to move. Was he mad at me?

"Hazel, drink. We want to look after you. After everything we just did, and with everything we *hope* to do, you need to stay hydrated," Zak warned. A small fire lit within me at his command. I don't know why, but Ronan was the only one who could order me about like that and get my immediate submission. When Zak tried it, I wanted to rebel, I wanted to push back and see what it took to ruffle that fun-guy exterior of his.

"I'm not thirsty," I lied.

Zak's grip on my thighs tightened and a little thrill ran through me at the fire in his dark eyes.

"You *will* drink that water," he growled low.

"No," I replied, very aware that my voice was breathy, but unable to strengthen it. Anticipation mixed with excitement, and I found myself wanting to push him further.

"Drink, or I will punish you."

"No, you won't," I dared. He cocked an eyebrow and slid a hand between my legs, teasing my wet entrance. I gasped and tried to lower myself over his seeking fingers, but he slid them away, making it impossible to impale myself on them.

"Drink."

"No," I retorted immediately, feeling myself pulse and throb at the idea of defying this man.

His fingers stroked me again, over, and over, bringing back that fire inside me. I rocked against his palm and was glad when he didn't pull away this time. He pulled me tighter against him, and I could feel his cock hardening again, pressing upwards along his stomach. I moaned and leaned forward to kiss him, and he urged my hips forward, to grind against him.

How? How was it possible for me to want to come a third time in less than two hours? I'd never come more than once in a night, two had been a staggering surprise. But here I was, riding my way towards a third.

"You want to come, baby girl?" Zak whispered against my mouth.

"Yes," I whispered unsteadily.

"Yes, what?"

"Yes, sire. Please, I want to come," I almost begged, feeling it build and build, knowing it was going to send me to a level of pleasure I had been lacking in my life.

I was almost there when Zak pushed me backwards on his thighs and away from his hard cock.

I panted and looked down at him, confused. "What? Why?"

"Drink," he ordered, his chest rising and falling faster now, his cheeks flushed.

"Zak!" I complained. A sharp slap landed on my backside, and I gasped.

"What did you just call me?" he growled.

"Sire," I corrected quickly.

"That's my girl," he whispered and brushed his thumb over the stinging flesh. I shivered at the combination of sensations. "Do you want to come? Do you want me to help you get there?" he asked, gently rubbing his fingers against my throbbing clit again.

"Yes," I answered with a trembling voice, my head falling back, my hair tickling my bare back.

"You want to come for me, baby girl?"

"Yes, sire," I begged, rocking harder against him, feeling it build and build. He pulled me close to him, letting me grind against his rock-hard cock to ride myself to a screaming crescendo—

"No!" I almost sobbed when Zak pushed me away again.

"Drink. Your. Water," he warned breathlessly, enunciating each word with a bite in his tone. I could tell this was torture for him, that he wanted desperately to come too.

"And if I don't?" I asked, my determination to play with him waning in the face of missing out on a world-rocking orgasm.

"Then I will continue to bring you close to the edge and never let you fall over it," he warned.

"You wouldn't."

"I would."

"You can't," I rephrased.

"I can and I will if you continue to fight me on the things that are good for you," Zak snapped.

I studied his face carefully for a moment, and something in it told me he wasn't lying. Where most men couldn't get a woman off when they tried, Zak not only knew how to get a woman there, but he also knew how to keep it from her as well.

That was a *sucky* punishment.

"Fine," I ground out. I was thirsty anyway, and some part of me didn't mind losing this little battle of wills. Zak's smirk was contagious, and I watched as he unscrewed the water bottle and handed it to me. The look of approval in his eyes made fighting him on the issue that much sweeter. I took several mouthfuls, not realizing how thirsty I was until that moment. A couple of drops fell onto my chest, and I sucked in a sharp breath at the feel of something so cold on my heated skin. I lowered the water bottle and sighed in satisfaction as I felt Zak lick up the drops. Without lifting his head, he took the bottle from me and put it back on the side-table before he dragged me close to him and urged me to move against him.

"You're not going to make me stop this time?" I asked, my voice wavering, not sure if I could survive it again.

"No, baby girl. You earned it," he assured. I smiled in relief and let myself get lost in the build-up again, secure in knowing he wouldn't take my pleasure from me again.

"Zak," Ronan's voice snapped. I paused, panting, and we both turned to look at him. He was frowning in disapproval. "She's sore; she should not be having sex again right now."

"I'm not inside her, Ronan," Zak assured roughly as he urged me to keep moving. "She's grinding on me. I have denied our girl an orgasm several times because she refused to drink her water. She's finally done as she was told, and now she needs a reward." Being called their girl sent another spasm of pleasure through me and I bit back a whimper. My gaze was locked on Ronan as I started moving again, and I watched the desire in his eyes escalate.

Zak turned my head towards him, and he was kissing me, his tongue tangling with mine as I rocked against him faster.

"Good girl, Hazel. Come again, baby. Ride me," Zak moaned. I could feel him so hard against my clit, but he wasn't trying to slide inside me. He was determined to help me get off, but not if it meant hurting me.

"Shit, baby. I want to tie you to my bed and fuck you for a week. Would you let me, Hazel? Would you let me keep you as my captive and sink my cock into you any way I wanted it?" Zak moaned, gritting his teeth.

I gasped and nodded.

"Answer me, baby," Zak ordered.

"Yes, sire," I answered, willing to agree to anything in this moment.

"You like the idea of being helpless, don't you, baby? Do you want us to use your body to get off, to keep you helpless for our pleasure, to fulfill our desires?" Zak groaned, his harsh whispers only sending me closer and closer to the edge. Knowing Ronan was there watching, getting harder seeing us do this on the couch added a deliciously naughty element to it all.

"Yes," I whimpered. I was so close.

"Yes, what?" Zak demanded, spanking me sharply.

"Yes, sire."

"That's a good girl. Now use my dick to come, baby. You're almost there," Zak groaned, his fingers digging into my ass as he urged me along, faster, harder.

I moaned as I got closer, my eyes closing, my head falling back as I gripped Zak's shoulders harder, my nails digging in, my toes curling as the pressure built and built—

"Yes!" I cried out, grinding harder against him, my head spinning and my heart pounding as it crashed over me. It was a real possibility that I'd gone deaf, died, or passed out. Nothing around me seemed to exist for some infinite amount of time; only pleasure, only bliss. I'd had orgasms before, but *nothing* compared to that one.

"Fuck, you're beautiful when you come," Zak praised, bringing me back to the here and now as he dipped his head to suck one nipple and then the other. I shuddered against him, feeling the last of my orgasm wash over me before I slumped forward.

My gaze rose slowly to meet Ronan's and he smirked.

"You did so good, Hazel," he whispered. "Zak, we should talk to her first about what she wants to do before we do them. Withholding orgasms and forcing them are on that list," Ronan reminded, only a small reprimand in his voice.

"I know," Zak answered, ducking his head. "I should have asked first."

"There's a list?" I asked. Ronan gave me a kind smile and nodded.

"We'll talk about it after your bath," he assured. Nodding, I watched as he turned around and left the room. I figured he was still organizing the bath.

I didn't want to move, I felt like jelly, my bones non-existent after three explosive orgasms. My eyelids were droopy, and if a meteor came down from the skies and obliterated us all right there, I would have died a happy woman.

"You know, we don't expect you to do anything more tonight," Zak began softly, tracing his hand up and down my bare back. I mustered up my strength and pulled away, dread beginning to weigh down on me. "If all you want to do after your bath is go to sleep, or go back to your hotel room, that's going to be okay with us," Zak stated, and he sucked down half of the water in his bottle.

My heart sank a little and disappointment weighed on me.

"Oh. Okay... umm, I mean, if you guys would prefer me to go back, I can do that. It... I don't want to make you guys uncomfortable in your own place, and I certainly don't want to come off as some clingy hookup," I answered quickly, shuffling back on his lap, suddenly aware that he was still naked, and I was in nothing but a flimsy thong.

"What? No, Hazel, you have the wrong idea," Zak hurried to assure me, but I felt so stupid. Here I was thinking this was going to be one of those epic nights, but I was turning out to be the clingy hookup that wouldn't leave their apartment. Humiliation stung my cheeks, and I was almost completely off Zak's lap when he gripped my hips and dragged me forward again.

"Baby girl," he whispered, and I shook my head. I pushed against his chest, trying not to be distracted by the inked skin in front of me as I kept my eyes averted.

"Are you going to refuse to look at me?" he asked softly.

"Yes," I mumbled. Zak cupped my face and waited until I met his chocolate gaze.

"Baby, after the tiny taste of you I have already had, if I thought I could convince you to stay in my bed for a week, I would do it. I don't want you to go, believe me, I just didn't want you to feel stuck or obligated. I needed to make sure you know that in everything we do, you have choices, even when we pretend you don't," he insisted.

I frowned. "When would we pretend I don't have choices?"

I wanted to believe he wanted me like that; I really did, but I'd been betrayed by the man I planned to marry and my best friend of over a decade. I wasn't feeling all that irreplaceable right now. Zak's grin was slow and sexy, and an answering heat sprung to life in my core.

"It's sometimes sexy to pretend, and sometimes it's freeing to allow yourself to be restrained during sex. Like... maybe you're tied to the bed because I broke into your house, and I decided to have my wicked way with you. And that perhaps—at first— you'd put up a small fight, but you realize that you want this, you want what I'm doing to you, and even though you know it's wrong, you don't want me to stop. So, I keep you tied up so that you can't move, so that you feel safe in thinking you had no choice but to accept the pleasure I gave you, but deep down, you wanted it," he explained in a low voice that sent heat curling inside me.

"Woah," I breathed, finding it all too easy to picture that scene. His grin widened.

"Or... possibly your father owes Ronan and me money, and we decided to take you as payment instead. Maybe Ronan would decide what we do and when we do it, and you'd have no choice but to take it and like it," he tempted roughly.

I leaned into him, feeling his fingers knead the sore muscles back there.

Holy hell... was this really who I was? Was I the girl who got turned on by scenes of reluctant sex or dubious consent?

"Mmm... Hazel, are you getting turned on again?" he whispered, slowly leaning forward to kiss me. I met him halfway, almost desperate to kiss him, the scenes he described alive in my mind.

"Come on, baby girl. Let's get you in that bath before you fall asleep," Zak suggested, almost as breathless as me. I nodded, unable to walk. I closed my eyes as Zak stood with me in his arms, and carried me towards the bathroom. I had a brief moment of satisfaction when I realized Zak was carrying me, and he did it as if it was no effort at all.

Richard sucked.

I lifted my head when I saw the bath was filled with hot water and bubbles. Ronan had even gone so far as to light some candles.

"I'm going to put you down here, baby girl. Enjoy your bath, take all the time that you need," Zak said softly, gently placing me on my feet.

"Thank you."

He leaned forward to kiss me again, winked, and then exited the bathroom, his erection still pointing upwards. I smiled at the dimples in his ass and then lifted my gaze as Ronan walked in. He placed a towel and a change of clothes on the basin edge along with another water bottle.

"Soak for as long as you need. I want you to drink some more water. You need it," Ronan told me. I pondered how when Zak told me to drink water I wanted to fight back, but when Ronan said it, I was thirty seconds away from kneeling before him to do whatever he desired. Why did I feel so different with each man? I stepped in closer to Ronan when he kept some distance and his eyes widened as I leaned up to kiss him, barely remembering that I was practically naked.

"Thank you, Ronan.

"I told you Zak and I wanted to take care of you. I didn't just mean have you sexually satisfied," he answered. I smiled then and he leaned forward to kiss me, slowly, gently. When we pulled away, he pressed another kiss to my forehead and stepped away.

"Get in the bath. If you're not out in an hour, I'm going to come looking for you to make sure you didn't fall asleep. Do you need anything else?" he offered. I shook my head.

"I'm good, thanks."

With another small smile, Ronan closed the door behind him, leaving me alone in the bathroom.

CHAPTER TEN

The bath was excruciatingly delicious on my sore muscles.
I winced slightly when the hot water touched sensitive skin, but
then groaned and sank into it, momentarily limp in the heat that
enveloped me. The water had a pleasant scent to it; Ronan had to
have put something in it. I leaned back and allowed myself a
minute of blankness, a small measure of time where I was not
thinking about anything and simply enjoying the feel of heat
seeping into exhausted muscles and the feel of warm water
lapping at my skin.

But thoughts of what I had just done would not be kept at bay for
long. I could still feel him—*them*. Oh, God, I had just allowed
two men to see me naked, to touch me, to kiss me, to—
My face burned at the memory of them; the strokes of their
hands, the rough murmur of their dirty words whispered against
my lips and in my ear; the hard, heavy thrusts of Zak as he fucked
me on Ronan's lap.

I slid under the water for a moment, fully submerging myself and
closing my eyes as if that would banish the truth from existence.
But it didn't. If anything, it made it worse. I could feel them
more acutely than ever; hear Zak's low grunts of pleasure as he
took me from behind; hear Ronan's dark commands and praises
as I let Zak have me while Ronan watched. It was like I could
hear my own whimpers, my pleas, my moans, and the way I'd
called Zak sire, and Ronan sir.

I came sputtering to the surface of the water, wiping at the liquid
as it rushed from my face. Who was this woman who wore my
face but wasn't me?

"But you like it, don't you?" Ronan's whispered words came back to me. *"You like hearing that you're being a good girl. I see it in your face every time I say it."*

I *had* liked it. The way they looked at me, it was with utter adoration. The way they touched me, even when they were rough, was like I was something special, something precious. They were kind, considerate, and utterly determined to give me pleasure above all else, even their own. Both of them took my safety and comfort seriously. They'd given me multiple chances to leave, and had made sure I knew how to get out of any situation if I wanted it to stop. The two of them had assured me that no matter what, if I said the word, they would stop whatever we were doing. Neither had made me feel like I was stuck or unable to leave. They'd gone out of their way to make sure I knew I could stop it at any point.

I really could get caught up in the vision these two incredible men set out before me if I wasn't careful.

I could still feel Ronan, the way he'd brushed his lips over me, the way his dark eyes searched my face, the way he paid attention to what made me gasp, moan, and squirm. It was like he was detailing every way there was to drive me wild, and he hadn't even slept with me yet.

Yet.

I mean... it was *yet*, right? I wasn't going to leave here without sleeping with him too, was I?

I groaned. Oh God, listen to me! *Sleep with him too*?! Who was this woman?

I sat in the bath, frowning, waiting for horror and regret to settle over me, maybe even shame and humiliation... but they didn't come. Knowing everything I'd done, I was shocked at myself, yes, but I was also... elated. Being with Zak and Ronan had been the most liberating experience of my life. It had taken me somewhat out of myself and shown me that I was capable of so much more, that I was *worth* so much more.

Two men I barely knew had made me feel more treasured, more protected, more desirable and wanted in two days than my fiancé or family had ever done in my entire life. That kind of intensity, that kind of devotion and desire was something I could let myself get used to.

But I couldn't, and I shouldn't.

They weren't offering forever; they were simply offering tonight and maybe another night or two. But this would all end because they would move onto their next conquest, and I would go back to my boring, vanilla life… wouldn't I? Wouldn't they?

"You like hearing us speak to you, telling you how hot your body is, how it feels to fuck you, to taste you."

It was Zak's words that echoed in my head this time and my breath caught in my throat. I did like it, I craved it… I wanted it more than anything else right now. No one had ever spoken to me like that in my entire life. They had been brutally honest, egos aside. It was as if they *needed* to tell me, needed me to understand how they saw me, and how they felt about me. They needed me to know.

And what did that mean for me?

"…it also means you're meant for more than the vanilla lifestyle you'd been living. And if you'll let us, we want to show you how much more there is to enjoy."

On shaky limbs, I climbed out of the bath, dried off and dressed in the shirt Ronan had given me. I didn't bother with the pants, they were too large anyway. Giving myself time to think, I took longer to dry my hair, and then wiped away the remnants of makeup before giving myself a quick mental check over. I was a little sore, deep inside, but in a way that kept the heat in my cheeks and a smile hovering on my lips the entire time. The bath had done wonders to eliminate all my other aches and twinges. I looked at myself in the mirror, expecting not to recognize the woman looking back. But all I saw was me, as if the woman I had always been was finally staring back at me without all the layers of everyone else I'd tried to be over the years.

The heartache and hurt I expected to feel at Rich's betrayal was still absent. At first, I had thought it was the shock, that the reality of what he'd done hadn't sunk in. But I was able to feel the sting and hurt at my friend's betrayal, so why not at his? I had been engaged to be married, for heaven's sake. Surely, I should be feeling more than humiliation and stupidity at being duped... shouldn't I? Had I even loved the man? Or had I simply accepted him as my co-star in the play I'd been starring in my entire life? The more I thought about it, the more I realized my feelings for him had been as superficial as my relationship with my parents. I cared for them, but I was just playing a role, reading my lines, and doing my duty. Emotion had been there on the surface for Rich, but deep down where I was supposed to have felt it, there was nothing. As for my best friend? Well... that was an ache too deep and raw for me to look at right now. I wanted to forgive, but the memory of what I'd seen, the stabbing realization of what I'd been overlooking, the lance of pain that had shot through me at finally understanding... I dropped my head forward, shaking off the baggage that came with that memory.

Right now, I had *two* stunning, strapping, utterly incredible men waiting outside that door for me who were determined to give me unparalleled pleasure, and I wanted to make the most of it before they told me it was time to leave.

Taking in a deep breath, I hung the towel up and slowly opened the bathroom door, but I stopped before exiting. I could hear deep voices from the kitchen and paused when I heard my name. "We need to be careful, Zak. Hazel isn't used to this," Ronan was saying.

"I know. It's painfully obvious, but Christ, Ronan, the way she responds, the way she moves... I don't know what's harder; my cock or the restraint I need not to take everything she's offering all at once," Zak replied.

A glow of warmth spread across my chest, and I bit my lip.

"I know, and I haven't even been inside her... yet. If she'll let me," Ronan continued.

"Why wouldn't she let you? I saw the way she looked at you, the way she responded to you," Zak replied. Frowning, I pressed closer, wanting to hear this too.

"I'm... different. You know that. I'm not sure she'll like the way I do things in bed. Besides, she's been in there for almost an hour now. I'm not sure she'll come out and want to continue. I'm fully prepared for her to tell us she wants to go home. I mean, this is not her usual thing. Maybe now that she's had some time alone to think, she's reconsidered staying for the night," Ronan answered.

There was a small silence, and I found myself holding my breath, waiting for Zak's response. And what did he mean when he said he was different in bed? What more did he need to enjoy sex?

"I don't think she's going to leave. You didn't see her dejection when she thought I was nicely trying to shove her out the door. She was hurt, disappointed. She wants to stay, Ronan," Zak assured, and I smiled, glad he understood.

"Maybe... but she'll only stay one night," Ronan responded, and I frowned at the small note of regret and acceptance in his voice.

"You don't know that. She might decide to stay... if we ask," Zak answered.

Something like hope sprung to life inside me, and I wondered at that. Did I want them to ask? Would I really consider staying more than a night? If I did, then this went beyond simple experimentation. This delved right into acceptance of a new lifestyle, a new me. Or maybe it was finally acceptance of the real me.

"I'm not so sure of that. Even if she agreed, I'm not sure that's a good idea," Ronan returned, and I tried not to be hurt by his response. A tense silence followed before Zak spoke.

"She's not Taylor, Ronan. If you haven't noticed, Hazel is very different, and I don't think she'll treat you like Taylor did. I think she's more accepting than that."

My curiosity piqued. Who was Taylor? What did she do? What was so bad that she didn't accept?

"If Hazel wants to stay the night, and wants me to be with her, then I will take what she's giving," Ronan responded, his tone guarded.

"But you won't ask her for what you really want in bed, will you? You won't let her see what you're like." The way Zak said it made me think he already knew the answer.

"It's better this way for all of us. You remember how it turned out last time."

My heart hurt at the pain in his voice. I was also worried... What did he want that would make another woman hurt him in her rejection? And what was so worrisome that he wouldn't ask it of me now?

I turned my head and caught sight of myself in the mirror. Could I be brave again and ask him to be himself? Could I do this for the man who had given me such a gift already?

Stiffening my spine, I gently closed the door and made a show of opening it, sure to make noise so they knew I was coming.

As I stepped out into the cooler room, both men came out of the kitchen, and the way their eyes dipped to my bare legs and dragged up my body, heating with appreciation, made my cheeks fill with heat again. Good lord, a woman could get used to being

HER SIR & SIRE

looked at like that.

"The pants were a little long, and I don't like to wear them in bed if I don't have to," I explained softly.

"I like to sleep naked," Zak announced with a grin.

"That won't bother me at all," I said quickly, making it known that I was staying.

Ronan's intense brown gaze met mine, seeking, reading, looking for God knows what, but I hoped he found it. I smiled and gnawed on my lower lip.

"So, uh... you guys have given me a word to use if I want things to stop," I began. Zak stiffened ever so slightly, and I watched Ronan's gaze shutter, preparing for rejection. Neither looked mad, only that they were bracing themselves for the inevitable.

"We did," Ronan answered deeply.

I nodded and sucked in another breath. "Is there a word to use if I want to move things forward? Get things started... maybe kick them up a notch?"

There was a small, stunned silence, and then Zak grinned and shook his head, chuckling softly under his breath as he raked a hand over his head in relief. Ronan's dark eyes never left my face, but the heat in them should have turned me to a pile of hot ash.

"What do you want to do, love?" Zak asked when Ronan remained silent, watching me.

"I want to try something new. I want to be pushed more," I replied, my voice an unsteady whisper and my knees slightly shaky.

"What do you want?" Ronan asked, stepping forward. Sucking in a breath, I stiffened my knees, refusing to back up or let them buckle. My heart was pounding, my mouth was dry, and my core was throbbing in anticipation. I had no idea what I was asking for, no idea what they'd have in stock for me. But I also knew, no matter how hard, no matter how scary they could appear, both of them would rather die before hurting me, before forcing me to do something I wasn't comfortable with.

Ronan's dark brown eyes were scorching, burning. I licked my lips quickly and his eyes followed the movement before gradually dragging up to my eyes.

Holy shit.

"I want you," I whispered, my nipples hardening beneath the shirt.

If I had thought Ronan's eyes were dark before, it was nothing compared to now.

"You want my cock, little girl?" he breathed, his shoulders held ridged with control.

"Yes. Please, sir."

Ronan growled low, it was a rumble in his chest that caused heat to pool low and my thighs to squeeze in anticipation. He slid his hands around my waist and pulled me tight against him, his large hands wide across my back as if he were trying to cover as much of me as possible.

"Do you want me to fuck you, Hazel?" he asked, his voice gravelly. I searched his piercing stare, making sure to look him when I replied.

"I want you to take me however you want me. Don't hold back because you're concerned you'll frighten me."

I felt his breath catch, his rigid body taught and barely controlled. There was a fine tremor that ran through him as he stared at me with burning desire and a sliver of reservation. I slid my hands up his arms to link behind his neck as I pushed myself up on my toes, my lips an inch away from his.

"I want you, Ronan. I want to know what it is like to be with *you*. The real you."

He swallowed, something like hope burning in his eyes, but he blinked, and it was gone.

"Hazel," he began, his voice a low warning, but I shook my head. "I want to try new things; I want to see what is out there. I am a clean slate, hardly touched. I don't know what I like or what I'm missing. But you, Ronan, I feel that you and Zak are just the men to show me, and I don't want you to protect me from it. I want you to show it all to me," I continued. He stared unblinkingly, a predator watching his prey.

"You don't know what you're asking," he tried to warn, and I shook my head.

"Then show me. I need to see the real you, Ronan. All of it," I whispered. Uncertainty shone back at me through his eyes, warring with hope and desperation.

They were helping me to find myself, helping me to live a life outside the protective bubble I'd grown up in. I was becoming my own person, and it was all because of them. I wanted to help Ronan be unafraid to ask for what he wanted, to take it without fear or rejection.

"You remember the word, sweetheart? The word to protect you?" he rasped. I nodded. "Because, baby, this is going to be a scenario where the word *stop* is not going to work. You have to be sure, Hazel. You are safe with me, always safe. I will never force you, even if it seems like I am. You say the word, and I stop immediately, even if I am seconds from coming."

"I know, and I remember the word," I assured

"I mean it, sweetheart. Do not keep going because you're scared of what we'll do or how we'll react. If you don't want it or you need things to stop, say the word. I'll never forgive myself if you ever push yourself past what you want to do because you're scared of me. I'll never be mad at you for stopping the scene. Promise me," he growled, and I could feel the way he rocked against me, his control slipping, but he was desperate to make me understand, to make sure I knew and felt safe. My heart did that melting, fluttering thing again and I marveled at how safe and cherished I felt.

"I promise, Ronan. If I need you to stop, I know what word to say. Even if I say stop, I promise I don't mean it. I can play along. If I really mean it, I'll say *vanilla* just like you asked," I promised, repeating the word so he knew I remembered it.

Another long, tense moment passed, and he seemed to be struggling with himself, some inner war raging that I was not privy to.

Come on, Ronan. Be brave with me.

CHAPTER ELEVEN

Ronan closed his eyes for a moment, his hard shaft pressing against me. God, he had to be in pain with how hard that thing was.

When he opened his eyes again, they were glittering down at me with a dark craving—heated and scorching. He was still Ronan, but he was somehow *more*. It reminded me of that subtle change I'd noticed down at the bar when I'd refused to drink the water. He seemed larger, and he took up more space; everything about him radiated power and control.

It was intoxicating.

There was a hunger on his face that whispered of forbidden needs and wants. His hands slid up my waist to my shirt and he slowly unbuttoned it, never once taking his gaze from mine. I saw Zak move to stand beside me from the corner of my eye. He brushed a kiss over my neck, goosebumps erupting up my arm and making my nipples ache.

"No matter what, you're safe, baby girl. Always safe with us," he breathed against my neck before he bit me there. I shuddered in reaction, and he grinned and moved past us to the bedroom. I refused to look away from Ronan. I shivered slightly when my shirt fell from my shoulders to pool in a pile at my feet. My skin was sensitive, my nipples hard, and my thighs wet with anticipation.

Ronan took my hands and pulled them around to my lower back where he circled them both with one hand.

His other hand came up slowly to wrap around my throat. My heart pounded hard, and my breath picked up in anticipation. The entire time, he never looked away from me, never blinked. I think he was trying to gauge my reaction to each movement, but I was hot as hellfire.

"Struggle," he whispered roughly. I blinked, dumbfounded, and his jaw clenched. "Fight me, Hazel. Put up a fight."

I swallowed hard, understanding dawning. He liked to dominate; he liked to press his woman into submission. A quiver worked its way up my spine and my pulse pounded between my legs at all the delicious images that appeared inside my mind.

I started by trying to regain control of my hands, but his grip on my wrists tightened and I watched his eyes flare with delight.

"Let me go," I breathed, my voice shaky.

His hard cock twitched in his pants. "No," he growled, walking me backwards.

I struggled some more, trying to break free, but his grip never loosened and his hand around my throat tightened. I was shocked at the thrill of excitement that went through me at that. He wasn't blocking my airway, he was compressing the sides of my neck, restricting blood flow, and it was delicious.

"Let me go," I said again, louder this time, fighting back harder. His jaw flexed and his eyes almost glowed in the dim lighting. We'd made it to the bedroom now and a small lamp was lit, setting the room awash in a warm glow. Ronan spun me around, quickly regaining control of my wrists that were now pinned between my back and his hard cock, his hand back on my throat. I could see Zak there on the bed, naked, sitting up and waiting. His dark eyes were burning as they watched us, searching my face. I knew a part of him was looking to see if I was panicking, if I was unsure, but I wanted this. I made sure to send him a reassuring smile before I struggled again. Zak's lips curled in a slow smirk, and I feigned a whimper.

"Let me go!" I cried out, struggling harder. Ronan had to grip my wrists almost painfully, his hand on my throat tightening.

"Now, now, princess, you're ours for the night. You came here to pay off your husband's debt, and we get to use you in any way we see fit," he growled low, putting the scene into my head.

Oh, they wanted to roleplay. I'd never done that, and I wasn't sure how to continue. A slow wave of heat engulfed me, and I was sure my face was hot. I was embarrassed, but when Zak's hungry eyes looked me over from head to toe and back again with the atmosphere in the room crackling around us, I decided I didn't care. I wanted this so bad.

"Just for one night, Ronan? That'll only give me enough time to eat that pretty pussy before I'm ready to move on to anything else," Zak replied, his voice low and velvety. My knees knocked, my breath hitched, and my nipples hardened.

Woah.

"She might like it enough to agree to work off a little more debt," Ronan replied.

"No, please. Let me go. I don't want to do this," I whispered, playing along, a part of me feeling stupid. When neither of them stopped, I was relieved. They trusted me to say the word if I really wanted it to end. Everything else said in the meantime was for the scene we were in.

"We're going to fuck you so hard you won't be able to walk for a week," Ronan growled against my ear, and I felt more wetness coat my inner thighs.

Holy. Shit!

Without pause, Ronan shoved me closer to the bed before he almost threw me onto it. Zak grabbed me, twisting me over until I was on my back, and he rested over me.

"Hold still, baby, you'll like this," Zak demanded as he nipped my neck, my chest, taking his time to suckle hard on both nipples. I arched my back and whimpered, then remembered I wasn't supposed to give in so easy.

"Stop," I insisted, pushing at his head, trying to twist away.
Ronan stepped to the side of the bed, and I looked up at him. He
leaned forward and grabbed my wrists, holding them down
beside my head.

"Easy there, sweetheart. We're going to make you feel good," he
rumbled.

"No, I don't want this," I pleaded, surprising myself at how
genuine I sounded.

"Too bad. You owe us, and now you have to hold up your end.
Now shut up before I stuff my cock in your mouth and make
you," he snarled. I tried to press my thighs together as a
pounding, pulsing ache thrummed through me and came to stop
at my clit.

Fuck.

"Your skin is so soft, baby. So fucking soft," Zak practically
purred as he made his way down my stomach. I wanted to bury
my head in embarrassment when he yanked my knees apart and
buried his face against my crotch, inhaling deeply.

"Fuck... the scent of you drives me wild," he moaned.

"P-please," I whispered, rocking my hips. Zak chuckled low
against my lower abdomen and grinned up at me.

"I think the princess wants her pussy licked. Is that what you
want, baby?"

"Eat her pussy, Zak, and tell me how she tastes," Ronan
demanded, his voice rough like gravel. The sound of it had my
nipples pebbling painfully and his dark eyes skimmed over my
body to watch my face.

"You're ours, sweetheart, forever. You may as well get used to
it," he warned me. I was pretty sure it was wishful thinking on
my part, but that almost sounded like a genuine threat. A threat I
was more than happy to have thrown my way.

These two men? Forever? Where do I sign?

Suddenly, Zak buried his head between my legs and licked me over in one, long, deep, lick. I groaned, arching my back, but he threw his forearm over my hips to hold me in place. And then he ravaged me.

I had *never*, in my entire life, had someone go down on me like that. Rich had put his face between my legs twice in our entire relationship, and both times I'd felt like I was forcing him, and he was barely able to conceal his disgust for the act. He didn't seem to mind when I sucked him off though. All things considered...

I shook my head, banishing thoughts of Richard. I barely bit back another moan as Zak touched my opening with a single finger. He didn't push inside me, instead he traced around my opening, barely pressing down. It was driving me wild!

"No, no, please, you have to stop," I begged again, panting, straining to pull my arms away. Ronan held me tighter and leaned over me to suck hard on my breasts, taking a mouthful of flesh into his hot mouth like he was literally trying to devour my top half while his friend ate down below.

"Beg all you want, little girl, no one is coming to save you. Now, come on my mouth," Zak growled against me, the vibrations of his voice only sending me higher. Inhaling sharply, I opened my mouth to protest when he shoved two thick fingers inside me, causing me to cry out.

I gasped and panted in pleasure as he plunged his fingers into me again and again, his tongue and teeth doing things to me I didn't know they could do to a woman. Zak pressed down hard on my lower abdomen, not enough to hurt, and at the same time, curled his fingers up inside me.

I'd heard of people going deaf when they were too close to explosions, and I figured that must have been what happened when I came. One man tugging and nipping and sucking on my breasts, the other with his head between my thighs, his fingers driving in and out of me, stretching me, drenching me with the evidence of my own pleasure. I tensed and went rigid when the orgasm ripped through me, and it was several long, breathless seconds before I managed to start breathing again, but everything sounded partially muted, like I had wool in my ears.

"She's ready," Zak growled, and before I could even regain my wits, I was spun around so that my legs hung off the bed and Ronan stood over me. Zak took up the job of holding down my hands. Ronan gripped my knees and spread my legs wide and kept them parted. I felt exposed, vulnerable... and I didn't understand how it could be so damn hot. He was undressing, yanking his belt off and placing it on the bed before he kicked off his shoes and removed his socks. His pants followed and my gaze darted to the erection poking out of his black briefs.

"There has to be something else I can do," I whispered brokenly as I pulled against Zak's grip. He tightened his hold and yanked me further up the bed.

"There is," Ronan agreed as he jerked off his boxers, revealing the very long and hard length of him. I wanted to whimper, to groan. My heart was still hammering hard, my breath ragged and raw, and I was still shuddering from the earth-shattering orgasm I'd just had. Ronan was equal to Zak in size, maybe a little thicker, and he was so erect it made me all the more desperate for him.

"What?" I whispered, dragging my gaze back to his face.

"You can beg me to stop," Ronan rasped, wrapping his hand around his thick length, stroking from root to tip. My mouth went dry as I watched him fist himself, stroking over and over in slow, languid strokes. I'd never seen a man touch himself before.

"Stop?" I whispered dazedly.

"Beg me, Hazel. Ask me to stop, beg me not to fuck you with my cock. Plead with me not to bury myself in your hot little pussy and fuck you so hard you'll never get rid of the feel of me. Ask me not to come inside you," he growled, his eyes fierce and full of need. I swallowed hard, so turned on that I was likely to combust the second he touched me.

"Please," I whispered faintly, pulling against Zak's restraining hands again. "Please, let me go. Don't do this, please," I continued, watching the way Ronan gripped the base of his dick, his teeth gritting as if he had to restrain himself from coming. He crawled onto the bedspread, his shirt gone, and I got to witness the awe-inspiring ripple of muscles glide beneath his naturally tanned skin as he grabbed a condom from the dresser drawer. He sheathed himself in the thin latex and positioned himself between my legs.

"Touch her, Zak," Ronan ordered.

"No, don't," I hissed, shaking my head and trying to get up. Ronan gripped my knees and kept them spread far apart, his glittering eyes on my face.

Zak shuffled for a moment, and I gasped when I felt a soft material wrapping around my wrists. I looked over my head to see the restraints attached to the side of the bed where it had been carefully hidden beneath the mattress. I glanced at Zak who watched me. I wasn't sure I could get out of these on my own, but I knew the safe word; I knew how to make it stop. I had to trust them enough to listen... and oddly enough, I did.

Once my wrists were bound, Zak slid his hands around me to cup my breasts before he pinched my nipples. I cried out and he laughed low, almost cruelly.

"I think she likes it, boss. I think she wants it," Zak murmured, doing it again.

"She's going to be our perfect little fuck-toy for the night," Ronan agreed. Why, why, *why* did I like it when he said that? I ignored the question, not wanting to think too long about it right now.

"It was lucky her husband had such a pretty wife to bargain with," Zak added.

"My husband knows nothing about this, he'd never trade me for money to help him," I hissed, playing along.

Ronan grinned, pleased.

"Not only did he, but he requested we provide video proof as a receipt of this... repayment," Ronan explained. I paused for a second. Were they really videoing this? I wasn't sure I was okay with that.

"Just for the scene," Zak whispered against my ear. Relief struck me and I slid back into my helpless woman character.

"He wouldn't," I persisted.

"He did. I think your husband likes the idea of watching his princess getting fucked," Ronan groaned, stroking himself again. There was something wrong with me... because somehow, that was deliciously hot.

"Let me go!" I cried and Zak flicked my nipples again, brushing over them, circling them, rolling them between his fingers, all the while I felt myself get wetter and wetter, my core throbbing, desperate, ready for more. One of his hands gripped my throat and he squeezed gently, enough to send my eyes rolling back in pleasure. The other slid down my stomach and further down between my legs.

"Oh, baby girl," he groaned, his hard cock at attention and leaking pre-cum. "You're fucking soaked," he moaned, rubbing my clit in gentle circles, sending me higher.

"No," I whispered, but it was feeble, choked.

"I think the little princess likes us, boss," Zak continued playing the part, flexing his fingers on my neck.

"Make sure she's ready, Zak, because I can't be gentle," Ronan snarled low, and I glanced back at his face. It was etched into brutal lines of need and desperate, aching, pleasure. He was on edge, barely holding on. It was a little scary, if I'm honest, considering his size. But this was what I wanted—I wanted him. He was still holding back, afraid, desperate to protect me from his own desires. Seeing him kneel there, all gloriously bronzed skin, a large tattoo over his left pectoral and starting down his bicep, his dark eyes, full lips, and ragged breathing... it was a wonder I didn't come just looking at him.

Zak let up the pressure on my throat and I gasped.

"Just let me go, please. Don't do this," I pleaded, knowing my whispered cries would only make his grip on his control that much frailer. I knew they wanted me to enjoy myself, to find pleasure in their activities, but it had become a mission of mine to watch Ronan lose his precious control.

"I'm going to fuck you, little girl. After you come, I'm going to flip you over and fuck you from behind, and you're going to swallow Zak's cock," he groaned, gritting his teeth, his chest heaving. I swallowed at the image in my mind, both wanting it and being afraid of it. Zak and Ronan were big men.

"Looks like we might have to teach her a thing or two, boss," Zak added, catching my hesitation.

"She'll learn, if she knows what's good for her," Ronan rumbled. Zak's fingers between my legs got faster, a little harder and I tried to hold off. I was aching with the need to come, but I also knew Ronan wasn't there yet, he was still holding back.

"Please," I begged, allowing tears to sting my eyes. It wasn't hard. I wanted to come so bad that I felt like sobbing. "You're so big, you won't fit," I added, watching that tenuous hold slip more.

"Come for him, princess. Come on his fingers so you can be ready for my cock," Ronan demanded, his voice thick and rough. And that was it.

My back arched as the orgasm swept over me, my mouth open in a silent scream. And before I could draw in breath, I felt Ronan's shaft at my entrance, and he pushed himself inside me. I *did* scream then. Pleasure and pain crashed overtop of one another so that it was almost impossible to tell which I was feeling. My muscles clamped hard around him, and Ronan groaned, swore, thrusting hard. My body resisted at first, and I concentrated on relaxing as he forced his way inside. I didn't care; I just wanted him all the way in. I needed him there. I was desperate beyond anything I'd ever felt before.

Zak's fingers continued to work my clit, dragging out my orgasm so that stars danced before my eyes, and I found it hard to draw breath.

"Fuck, she's so fucking tight," Ronan snarled, gnashing his teeth.

"Oh, please stop!" I cried, and I watched victoriously as Ronan's hold on his control snapped. His expression twisted into something helpless, savage... and so *fucking* beautiful. He pulled out of me and slammed back in, over and over until he was fully inside me. Zak had edged back so Ronan had room to move, but one of his hands was still on my throat, the other now on my breasts, twisting and tugging, every stroke sending a fiery streak to my core.

"Fuck her, boss. Fuck her tight little pussy," Zak urged, his voice thick.

"That's it, princess. Scream for me," Ronan groaned. I screamed again and begged him to stop, all the while I was meeting his every thrust with one of my own, bringing my hips up to take him deeper, harder.

"Oh, you like that, don't you?" Ronan groaned and I spasmed around his cock again, feeling another wave begin to build. Why, oh why, did the fantasy have to make me so hot? I ignored that question too, not wanting to look too closely at what it said about me.

"You're close, princess. Come on my cock. I want to feel that pussy strangling my dick." Ronan growled his demand, his voice almost animalistic.

"Keep your legs spread, baby. Let Ronan fuck your sweet cunt," Zak encouraged, and my eyes rolled back again at his words. Shit, I was coming again.

"Yes! Yes, sweetheart, come on my cock," Ronan growled, his fingers biting into my hips as he surged in and out of me. My orgasm crashed over me, stealing my breath and I swear I almost blacked out. I was throbbing and aching, but Ronan wasn't done yet. His teeth were clenched as if he were holding off his own orgasm, his gaze glittering and dangerous.

"On your knees, princess. I want to fuck you while you suck on Zak's cock," Ronan demanded. I groaned and he pulled out of me, twisting me onto my knees. Shuffling up shakily, I held myself steady, my hands bound in front of me and not allowing for me to brace myself. I was held between Ronan with his grip on my hips and the material around my wrists pulled tight.

I glanced up at Zak who shuffled so that his crotch was lined up with my head and his legs spread out either side of me, the cord binding me drawn around his body. He pushed my hair out of my face and over to one shoulder, bunching it there at the base of my skull, his chest rising and falling rapidly in time with his harsh breaths.

"Suck my cock, baby girl," he ordered breathlessly.

I didn't, shaking my head in refusal.

Ronan growled, and with a swift, brutal thrust, he was back inside me, taking me from behind. I cried out, and as my mouth opened, Zak forced my face down and his shaft into my mouth. My throat tried to close, and he let me pull up slightly to breathe and find where I was comfortable. He was very good at seeming forceful without being so.

"Yes," Ronan groaned as he started to fuck me in earnest. I moaned at the feeling and Zak surged his hips up into my mouth, helping me to find the right rhythm.

"That's it. Good girl, Hazel. Suck my cock, just like that. You're so fucking beautiful with your lips around my cock. Such a good girl for letting Ronan fuck you like that," Zak grunted thickly. Hearing my name, hearing that praise just did something to me, and I clenched harder around Ronan.

I concentrated on not gnashing my teeth and keeping my mouth open without taking him too far. Zak was not a small man. I focused on timing my breathing as Ronan groaned and grunted behind me, his hips snapping hard and deep. The hand in my hair tightened and I felt Zack's thrusts get shorter and faster, his groaning telling me he was close.

"Boss?" Zak groaned.

"Come in her mouth, Zak. Take every drop of his cum, sweetheart," Ronan instructed. His voice was thick and harsh, almost guttural. He was rough, every stroke of his cock sent him deeper inside me. My jaw was beginning to ache, and I couldn't swallow around the massive length in my mouth. I felt dirty, used—why did I love it? The image we must have presented was animalistic. I was held between two men who were using my body to get off, using me to feel good. At this very moment, I was little more than a hot body to bring them pleasure, and for some reason, it made me feel desired and wanted... God, how did that even begin to work?

I moaned around Zak's cock, and he swore and thrust a little harder.

"Good girl, just like that. Suck harder for me, baby girl. I'm going to come in your mouth," he groaned, swearing, his grip on my hair almost painful now.

"I want you to come again, Hazel," Ronan snarled. Struggling, I
made a sound of dissent and Zak pulled my mouth off his cock.
"What was that, princess? Were you denying us?" he demanded,
stroking his engorged cock roughly with his other hand.

"I can't, it's too much," I panted, meaning it. I'd already come
more than once in the last half an hour, not to say anything of the
three orgasms earlier in the night; my body was wrung out.

"You can, and you will. Come on, sweetheart. Come one more
time on my dick. Give it to me," Ronan demanded, sliding his
hand around my front. I moaned, feeling raw and tired, but
Ronan's fingers were surprisingly soft, so different to the way he
was thrusting into me, and the way Zak's hand on my hair
tightened almost painfully as he pulled my face back down onto
his cock. I sucked on Zak, forced to take his length as he pushed
himself down my throat. I'd never been happier not to have a gag
reflex.

Hearing them moan, whisper their praises, and groan their
approval, combined with the scent of our sex, the sheer
naughtiness of this scene, it had me working up to another
orgasm.

"That's it, Hazel. Good girl. Get there. I can feel you. Give it to
me, sweetheart. Give me all of it, and don't you dare hold back,"
Ronan snarled, his voice guttural and desperate. My orgasm built
and built, impossibly bigger and harder than before.

"Come in her pussy, boss. Fuck her good and fill her up," Zak
rasped as I felt him swell impossibly in my mouth. He was about
to come, I could feel it, hear it in his voice as he moaned and
swore. I went to pull away, but Zak's hand kept me right where I
was.

"Fuck, fuck, fuck, *FUCK!*" Zak roared, and I felt hot streams of his
cum ejaculate into my mouth. He let me pull up slightly so I
wouldn't choke, and I closed my eyes and concentrated on taking

in every ropey spurt, trying to swallow quickly so that I wouldn't lose any. He was tangy, salty, a little bitter, but the act of taking his release in my mouth was so goddamn naughty that I didn't want to waste it. I didn't want to disappoint him in this fantasy. His legs shook beneath me, and he groaned, his grip on my hair loosening as he swore again, panting hard. I sucked on the tip of him a moment longer, and he shuddered, cursing.

"Fuck me, baby. You're amazing," he praised with a gasp.

Ronan moaned behind me and slapped my bare backside. I made a sound of surprise, my mouth pulling off Zak's cock completely. Another slap, this one harder, the sting sending warmth all across my rear end. Again, he spanked me, and again... six more times before I was screaming.

"Please, don't come inside me!"

Ronan slammed harder, sliding his hand around my throat and pulling me back so that I was almost sitting in his lap as he continued to fuck me.

"You're mine, sweetheart. This body is mine, this *pussy* is mine, and I will do whatever I damn well want with it. I'm going to come inside you, baby, and you'll fucking thank me for it," he growled, his voice purely animalistic. Oh God!

I moaned, gasping as he tightened his hold on my throat, ramming inside me so hard my breasts bounced, and pleasure bordered on pain. Tears stung my eyes as he powered into me, harder, faster, deeper. Over and over, his cock was driving inside me and all I could do was sit there and let him.

"Come on his cock, baby girl. Be a good girl and come for him again," Zak encouraged, and I opened my eyes with a sound of pleasure as he knelt before me and suckled a hard nipple into his hot mouth and began to rub at my clit with his other hand while Ronan fucked me harder.

"Yes, come on, baby, I can feel you. Give it to me, Hazel, let me feel you come on my cock again," Ronan ordered.

"No," I whimpered, my voice barely audible, and I was dangerously close to that edge.

"Yes," he snarled and his grip on my throat tightened. He began to swell inside me, his orgasm so close. I moaned, my head thrown back and Zak bit down gently on one nipple as a finger pressed hard on my clit.

Yes!

Back arched, air gone, I screamed my release into the dimly lit room, my inner muscles gripping Ronan's cock so tight I wasn't sure I would let him go. Ronan roared behind me and I felt him finally come, his body shuddering, his long, loud groan in the form of my name filling my ears and sending another round of pleasure through me. It went on and on, my pussy milking him for all he was worth, my lungs burning, my throat raw, and my body thoroughly used.

It was an eternity before Ronan stopped, his breathing labored, all of us a sweaty, panting mess. I gasped and puffed, struggling to remain upright. Stars danced before my eyes, my head felt light, my hearing muffled, and every part of my body wrung out with exhaustion. Zak carefully unbound my wrists, and I would have fallen forward had he not been there to catch me. He lifted my head, his thumbs wiping away the few tears that had streaked my cheeks, and there was concern in his eyes.

I smiled shakily and shook my head. "Please don't ask me if I'm okay. I might have to hurt you," I murmured drowsily, my voice a little rough.

He grinned in relief, his eyes flicking behind me for a moment before he nodded. I was going to assume he was letting Ronan know I was okay. Ronan slid from my body and the loss I felt was instant. I leaned into Zak, and he tipped my head back and fitted his mouth over mine in a soft, deep kiss. Sighing, I kissed him back, sinking against him and letting him take my weight. I was exhausted, my body tired, and so deliciously sore.

A moment later, Zak moved, and Ronan was there in front of me. I blinked slowly; my eyelids almost too heavy to lift.

"Hazel," he began, looking worried and regretful. He was still breathing heavily, Zak too.

"Please don't," I whispered huskily, and he blinked, frowning. "If you tell me you're sorry right now, I'm going to think that I wasn't enough for you, that I didn't go far enough, and that'll kill me. I loved every moment of that, every second, even the parts that scared me. Please don't tell me you're sorry."

I touched his jawline, sliding my fingers up to touch his lips. His eyes widened in surprise, and he studied me carefully, something like awe on his face and then he leaned forward to press his forehead against mine. He drew in several deep breaths before he pressed our lips together. I kissed him slowly, carefully, wanting to explore every part of him. A little bit of me got a thrill knowing he was kissing me when his friend had just had his cock in my mouth, had just *come* in my mouth, but that didn't seem to bother Ronan at all.

"You are the perfect woman, Hazel," he whispered roughly as he pulled away.

I was still trying to get my breathing under control, and I smiled drowsily. "I think you and Zak are God's gift to women... or maybe just to me," I responded. He grinned, a real, full-blown smile, and my heart twisted. Good lord, the man was gorgeous. Pride lit up within me, and I wanted to cheer at the appearance of his smile. I felt like I'd just won the lottery with that look alone.

"Let's get you cleaned up, baby girl," Zak said behind me. I gasped and pulled back from Ronan slightly when a warm cloth was pressed gently between my legs. I groaned, the heat of it reminding me of how much I was aching now.

"Did we hurt you? Did *I* hurt you?" Ronan asked, his voice deep and rough. I smiled gently and shook my head.

"It was rough, but I liked it. And it was so... so..." I was at a loss for words, and he smiled softly, almost sadly.

"Taboo?" he supplied.

"Yes... but I liked it," I admitted. His eyes searched mine, and I know he saw the questions I had, but he didn't answer them. He looked almost ashamed.

"What you like in bed, the scenes we play out, does not make you a bad person, Ronan," Zak said softly behind me, reading his friend perfectly. He removed the cloth between my legs as he spoke, and I watched Ronan close his eyes.

I framed his face with both hands. "Am I a bad person for liking what you did to me? For liking that scene... being forced?" I whispered, swallowing hard at the idea. His eyes hardened and his jaw tensed.

"No."

The answer was firm and stubborn, determined, and confident.

"Then you are not bad for liking it either," I reasoned. He searched my face and swallowed hard. Zak murmured something about getting a drink and left, and it was just Ronan and I on the bed, staring into each other's eyes.

"I... I struggle with it. I'd never in real life want to do something like that, but here in bed, where everyone knows the rules..." he explained, shrugging.

"It's different," I agreed. "I mean, I know I wouldn't enjoy that scene in real life. And I wouldn't enjoy the idea of my actual husband selling me or watching me... but somehow, in this fantasy..." I trailed off, my face hot, unsure how to properly explain it. He nodded, and I could see that he understood. Somehow, the fantasy was okay; it was hot, and it was allowed. We knelt on the bed together for some time, Ronan kissing me gently, brushing my hair back, studying me with fathomless eyes. What was he thinking? Did he regret this? Did I not do a good enough job? Was he truly worried I'd want to run away or call him a monster now?

"Do you want another bath?" Ronan asked after a few minutes of silence.

"I probably should," I hedged, the small twinges between my legs growing more pronounced, but I refused to show it. He frowned slightly, his gaze narrowing as if he'd caught it anyway.

"Bath, definitely," he murmured, almost growling. I grinned as he swept me up in his arms and carried me to the bathroom. I was glad that he did; I wouldn't have been able to carry myself had a gunman walked in and demanded it.

I was surprised to find the bath already half-way full. Really, I shouldn't have been—Zak and Ronan seemed determined to look after me in every way. While one tended to me physically, the other cared for me emotionally and by getting food or water or a bath. I was feeling very spoiled, cherished—desired.

"What about you two?" I asked as Ronan carefully placed my feet in the tub and helped me to stand on shaky legs. Zak ducked his head back in, his hair was still dripping and there was a towel around his waist.

"Already done for me," he answered with a grin. I smiled and Ronan brushed a kiss over my forehead.

"I'll have a shower when you get out. Are you hungry?" he asked. I shook my head and he frowned. Instead of arguing, he grabbed the water bottle I'd left in here earlier and handed it to me with a stern look. I rolled my eyes but smiled. He watched as I unscrewed the cap and took several large mouthfuls before I handed it to him. He raised an eyebrow and I waited. A smile tugged at his lips, but he took it and finished what was left.

"Get in the bath, and come out when you're ready," he

murmured quietly, kissing me once more before leaving me alone in the bathroom.

CHAPTER TWELVE

When I came out of the bath, Ronan made quick work of a shower and I walked into the bedroom to find my dress, shoes, and bag slung neatly over a chair. Zak took my towel from me and gently rubbed me down with it, taking special care to dry my hair. By the time that was done, Ronan was out. He was in a pair of gray sweatpants and a faded shirt, whereas Zak was in his briefs and nothing else. I'd moved to brush my own hair, but Ronan gently took the brush from my hands and sat behind me, carefully brushing out the snags and tangles. Zak leaned forward to kiss me and took one foot in his hand and began to rub it.

"Uh... what are you guys doing? Not that I mind," I said. Zak didn't answer right away, and Ronan cleared his throat.

"There are things we like to do for the woman in our bed once we're done People in our circle, with tastes like ours, there are things we need after sex," Zak finally answered.

"Okay?"

"There are some other names for it, but it's generally called *aftercare.* When playing the games we play, running the scenes we do and using the toys and techniques we know, there needs to be some care afterwards to make sure everyone is okay, that no one was pushed beyond their limits and that they enjoyed themselves," Zak began.

"Isn't that what the safe word is for?" I asked with a frown. Zak smiled gently and nodded.

"Yes. The safe word is to prevent anyone from going further than what they would like. But sometimes, like in the scene we just played, we need to be sure. In that scene... Ronan and I were forcing you, Hazel. We called you names and held you down, we forced orgasms and Ronan struck you. In regular life, we would never do these things. We know that it's wanted during this kind of sex, but when we come back to ourselves, when the scene ends, sometimes it's hard to come to terms with what we did. We need reassurance that we're not monsters," Zak continued.

I nodded slowly. I was pretty sure I understood, and I wanted to really think about what Zak was saying before I responded in case I offended them. I knew I'd pushed Ronan as much as he'd pushed me. It had almost been a compulsion. I had wanted him to lose control, and I'd wanted him to slip and just take me. It was important to make sure he knew he didn't do anything wrong.

"So doing things for me helps you?" I asked.

"Yes, it does. But we also happen to think you deserve these things, Hazel. If you…I mean, if you were to hang around, we'd do these things all the time, not just after sex," Ronan added softly.

My heart fluttered and I wanted to shake my head. Surely they were just saying that because they knew they'd never have to prove their word.

"So… are things always like that during sex?" I asked, turning my head slightly to look at him, wondering if thing always got so intense.

"No," Ronan continued with a small shake of his head. "I am known as a dominant. I need to be in control during sex, usually outside of sex too. My job is to know your limits and to not let you push yourself past them. I have this need to take my submissive over completely and rule her. I need her to submit to me."

"I got that," I whispered with a smile. Ronan's lips tilted at the corners, and he continued.

"Zak is known as a switch. He can go either way, be a submissive for the right dominant, or be a dominant for the right submissive."

"So, me... I'm a submissive?" I asked.

"Do you understand what a submissive is?"

I gnawed on my lower lip and shook my head. "I think I do, but you tell me," I answered.

"Many mistake a submissive for a servant or slave, someone with no willpower or backbone. It's not that way at all; although, playing the part of a servant or slave is satisfying for some submissives. They are the ones who give the dominants the power in the relationship by *allowing* themselves to be told what to do, when and how. You are the ones who set the boundary, and I'm the one who enforces it," Ronan explained.

"And this is just during sex?" I asked.

Again, the guys shook their heads. "Not always. Many people live the lifestyle all the time, and some just during sex. Liking to be dominated during sex is different to being submissive. Submissives *need* to be controlled and dominated, they need to be pushed to their limits and restrained from overdoing it or refusing to push themselves. They get a sense of peace, a rush of warmth, or a feeling of accomplishment when they do what they're being told to do," Ronan explained.

"And it's the same for you when you get to tell a submissive what to do?" I asked.

He shook his head. "My needs are met when my submissive does what I ask, not by giving the command. It's met when they do as I order, and then they are praised for it, and I can see that my command has met *their* need."

"So... then I *am* a submissive?"

"Before we answer that, I'd like you to try and answer it yourself," Ronan cut in before Zak could answer.

"How?" I frowned. Ronan stopped brushing my hair and moved beside me to look at me. He leaned in close and paused a hair's breadth away from my mouth.

"Kiss me," he whispered. I hesitated only a moment, watching his dark eyes as they drilled into me, the command in his voice clear. I leaned in and kissed him, unable to believe I was still enamored at the feel of his lips.

"Good girl, Hazel," he breathed as we pulled away. My chest warmed and I smiled softly at that shine in his eyes and the small tilt of his lips.

"Now tell me… do you think you are a submissive?"

Oh yeah.

I nodded, swallowing, and he smiled again, his eyes lightening. When Ronan took his seat again, I turned to look at Zak.

"So, you like to be both dominated and submitted to?"

"I am a switch, yes. But I won't simply submit to any dom. It has to be the right kind. They have to have a certain…" he trailed off, looking for the right word.

"Aura," I supplied, thinking about the way Ronan carried himself.

"Yes," Zak agreed, grinning at me. "She has to have the right aura. Unless you're a real dominant, you won't have that air about you, and it makes it hard to trust them in a sexual situation. I like dominating, especially to brats," he added.

I frowned. "What the heck is a brat?"

He smirked. "Do you remember earlier when you were refusing to drink the water, and I withheld your orgasms as punishment?"

I felt my face flush. Yes, I remembered. It was fun.

"That's being a brat. A brat is a submissive, but they like to taunt and tease and push their limits until they're pushed into submission. They still want to be praised like a sub, they want to submit, but they need to fight it first. I like handing out the punishments for not submitting, and the eventual reward," Zak answered. I nodded my understanding and considered what I'd learned.

"Hazel, do you know why you were being a brat with Zak?" Ronan asked softly. I opened my mouth to say no, but closed it, thinking hard.

"I guess... I guess there was just something about him that made me want to test his authority, to push him and fight with him to see what he would do," I answered.

"Do you feel that way with me?" Ronan asked.

I shook my head immediately, something in my stomach twisting at the thought of being that way with him. "No. Absolutely not."

"Can you explain?" Ronan asked. He looked curious, interested, and not at all bothered.

"I, uh... Zak makes me want to push him and tease him. He has a kind of playful air about him when I refuse. But you? Everything in me wants to do what you ask when you ask it. To say no to you feels... wrong. I need to do what you ask and..." I trailed off, my face heating.

"And what?" he asked, but his tone told me he already knew. I ducked my head and Zak tilted it up, smiling gently.

"There is nothing to be embarrassed about here, Hazel. We need to be able to talk about it all, remember?"

I nodded slowly and turned more to look at Ronan.

"I need your approval, Ronan. Whenever you ask me to do something, I need that look in your eyes when I do it. I crave your words when you tell me I did good or that I am good. I want it from Zak too, but I like the fight with him before he says those things. With you, I just need to... please you," I answered, confused at how happy it made me to need to do these things for another person.

"It's okay, Hazel. It's good. That is what a submissive does, what they want, and there is nothing bad about that," Ronan assured me.

"But it kind of feels... wrong. Like I'm sending women back to the eighteen hundreds," I muttered. Ronan laughed and shook his head, and my heart warmed at the sound.

"Look, being a submissive has many layers and many levels. Not all submissives are that way outside the bedroom, many aren't. There are a lot who need to be submissive in the bedroom because they are so in control during the rest of their lives. Being told what to do and when to do it, having all responsibility taken away for a few hours, it's a rush—a relief," Ronan explained.

"Well... I'm not all that controlling outside the bedroom," I muttered, thinking about how much my life had been planned for me.

"No," Ronan agreed thoughtfully. "But I think that's because you've never been given the chance. I think with some time you'll grow into your own person nicely."

I drew in a shaky breath and smiled softly, wanting to believe him, but I knew the truth. My whole life had been mapped to someone else's needs and wants. I'd never had control of it, not really.

"We know this is not your life, Hazel. But while you're here with us is there anything you think would calm you after a scene? Anything that you might need to ease back into yourself?" Zak asked after a silence. My heart skipped a beat at what him even asking that entailed. Were they asking in the anticipation of us doing this some more? Did they want me to stay longer? I mean, I was pretty sore, so I wasn't planning on any more happening tonight. And tomorrow? Well, I wasn't sure what I was planning to do then. But the fact they were asking meant they hoped there would be more, right?

"Can I touch you both?" I finally answered.

They each paused, and it was Zak who responded. "How?"

I shrugged. "I don't mean in a way to get you worked up again, but just... touch you. Maybe run my fingers through your hair," I said, leaning forward to do just that to Zak. "Trace your tattoos," I continued, moving to the shapes that started at his neck and worked my way down. I turned to look at Ronan.

"We'll make it happen," Ronan answered deeply. After a small pause I smiled, and Ronan cocked his head to the side. "What?"

"I... I think I'm going to keep baths on the list too. Maybe a few minutes to myself to breathe and soak. But otherwise, this is all I need to be okay with the two of you, to feel like myself, to sink back into who we all are," I replied. He smiled, his eyes alight with humor. He kissed me and turned me back around so that he could continue with my hair.

Sometime later, we crawled into bed, and I was surprised that both men climbed in either side of me.

"We both want to hold you," Ronan answered when I asked if one of them was sleeping on the pull-out couch. Happy to hear that, I rolled onto my side when Ronan pulled me in tightly, tugging one of my legs up over him. I smiled, wrapping an arm over his waist. Zak tucked himself in behind me, wrapping an arm around me. I was warm, I was exhausted and thoroughly pleasured. And never in a million years did I ever think I'd feel this safe within the arms of two men I barely knew.

"She's incredible," I heard Zak murmur just as I was on the edge of sleep, his voice at my back. I kept my body limp, which wasn't hard to do since I was so stupidly relaxed and made sure to keep my breathing deep and even.

"She's more than incredible," Ronan replied, his voice thick and husky, a rumble beneath my ear.

"She didn't fall apart, Ronan. She didn't tell us we were monsters. She didn't accuse us of rape or tell us we were sick," Zak continued. I wanted to frown but repressed the instinct.

"She... she just fell right into the scene, didn't she?" Ronan asked in a whisper; although I don't think he was looking for an answer.

"She is instinctual and picks up on what we need before we say it. She's a brat with you but a total submissive for me."

"She's perfect for us, you know that, right?" Zak asked, his fingers gently stroking my back.

"Zak... we can't," Ronan whispered in warning, tracing his finger up and down my arm stretched over his torso.

"Why not?" Zak demanded, and I could hear the restraint in his voice not to shout. There was a small silence.

"She has a life, and a family somewhere else. We're just an experiment to her, we're a small fling, a crazy ride on the wild side before she goes back," Ronan replied softly. I thought I could hear a sad resignation in his voice, but I could have been mistaken.

"What life? You heard her the other night. Her life is in shambles."

"Exactly. She's confused and vulnerable. She's not in the right state of mind to make decisions like that," Ronan replied, his hand gently squeezing my hip. What decisions?

"Ronan—"

"Plus, we barely know her. She's been here for two days, and one of those she was utterly trashed. We don't even know if we'd all get along," Ronan continued.

There was a small silence, and I reminded myself to stay limp.

"I can feel it, Ronan. I don't need to spend the next few months getting to know her to know she's meant to be ours. And you're lying to yourself if you don't admit that you feel it too," Zak whispered. Ronan tensed beneath me and sighed, his breath rustling my hair. His grip on my hip gentled, and he stroked the bare flesh of my arm. He was thinking, and I wondered if he was regretting our night.

"Zak... I don't want you to get your hopes up, not again. This is her first experience with this kind of life, and it's only been a night. She might be someone who only wants a taste, and not to make it her life. We need someone who understands and who needs things this way too, in and out of the bedroom," Ronan reminded softly.

"Look at how she responded to each of us tonight, Ronan. You *know* she understands and could do it. She even got you to lose your control, and that *never* happens," Zak pointed out.

"We can't push her, Zak," Ronan argued.

"Well... we could ask."

"Why don't we just see what she says in the morning? She might just want to go home," Ronan replied, his voice soft.

Did he sound... sad?

"I know you think I'm being rash, but I feel it, Ronan. She's meant to be with us," Zak murmured softly.

Ronan drew in a slow, steadying breath, and I felt him brush a kiss over my cheek again before his body relaxed beneath me.

Ours. As in, both of theirs... for good?

A tingle of warmth spread across my chest at the thought, and I sighed and snuggled closer to both of them. This was something I could think about tomorrow, because as much as I was tempted to agree with Zak's suggestion right now, I was in a post-orgasmic high that I had never experienced before, and Ronan was right. My life was a mess. I needed to figure some stuff out before I decided what I wanted to do with the rest of it.

CHAPTER THIRTEEN

The guys had been persuasive in getting me to stay in their bed for the weekend. Sure, they worked, and I helped out here and there, but for the most part, they kept me in their bed... or the shower... or the couch. I hadn't been lacking for orgasms longer than it took for me to get a few hours' sleep and then they were back at it again. It had been an incredible three days where I thought about nothing except the drop-dead-gorgeous men in front of me.

When I woke up on the fourth morning, it was to the feeling of intense pleasure.

"Good morning, baby girl," Zak groaned into my neck, his hard cock pressed against the seam of my buttocks, his fingers gently rolling and tugging at my nipples. I sighed at another continuing caress of pleasure, and I gasped, trying to squeeze my legs closed, but the wide pair of shoulders between them prevented it.

"Shh, just let Ronan make you come, baby," Zak whispered, his teeth grazing my shoulder.

I was on my side, Zak pressed against my back and his hands playing with my tender breasts. Ronan had shifted down, one of my legs was thrown over his shoulder, and his mouth was buried between my legs, his tongue lapping and spearing at my entrance. I blinked, my gaze lowering, and I caught Ronan's dark eyes peering up at me as he sucked. I moaned, my eyes closing as I gave myself over to the pleasure. Nothing was hurried, he kept at me like we had all the time in the world. Zak's fingers were gentle and stroking, bringing me slowly and unhurriedly to a crescendo of pleasure.

"You taste incredible, sweetheart," Ronan groaned against me, his tongue circling my clit, causing me to jerk against him, my breathing hitching. God, this had to be what heaven was like. "Good girl, just let it happen. Come on his mouth, baby," Zak groaned, rocking against me again.

Ronan's probing tongue and sucking mouth, Zak's stroking and tugging fingers, the whole situation where I was in bed with two stupidly hot, amazingly talented, strangely caring men at the same time while they both shared my body... I came. It wasn't a screaming, slamming orgasm like last night. It was soft, a gentle wave, intense in the build-up and pleasant in the crest. I arched, whimpered, my thighs automatically squeezing against Ronan. Zak kept my body pressed tightly to his as I gasped and came down, my brain a little foggy from pleasure but crystal clear after such a late night.

"You're fucking beautiful," Ronan mumbled against me, kissing the insides of my thighs, my abdomen and up to my breasts. He gently sucked on each nipple, and I arched against him before he kissed my neck and up to my lips. I opened my mouth to him, and he kissed me intensely, deeply, letting me taste myself. I didn't hate it... it was hot. When he pulled away, he kissed my cheek and then my nose and smiled lazily down at me.

"How do you feel this morning?"

"Relaxed, amazing... a little shy," I admitted, tugging the shirt back down.

"There's no need to be shy," he comforted. I knew that, but I couldn't help myself.

"I've never slept in so little when sharing a bed with someone else," I admitted.

"Not even your fiancé?" Zak asked with a raised eyebrow. I shook my head.

"No. I never got the feeling he liked my body, and so I always wore pajamas, even after sex," I explained, my cheeks warming as I focused on the tattoos of Zak's chest.

"He's a fucking moron," Ronan snapped behind me, his hands still stroking my thighs and my backside.

I bit back a grin and shrugged. "It's nothing to worry about."

"It is when it's damaged your self-confidence so much. I mean, fuck, Hazel. You're a goddamn knockout," Ronan argued strongly. I shook my head and Zak tipped my chin up to look at him.

"We mean it, baby girl, we're not just saying that. You are beautiful, sinfully sexy, and tremendously desirable. You are incredible, and it's a crime the man you were going to marry never made you see it, never made you aware of it," Zak told me, his dark eyes refusing to let mine evade him.

"I *want* to believe you."

"Then we'll have to make sure you do," he answered with a grin. I smiled and he leaned forward to kiss me again.

Hours passed as we lay in bed talking and getting to know one another. We moved beyond sex and into our childhoods and where we grew up. I left a few things out, like the white supremacy of it all; I didn't want to risk scaring them away just yet. Their questions and comments had me laughing so much my stomach hurt, and I felt twenty feet tall every time I got Ronan to laugh. Watching him and Zak interact was interesting, seeing how they fit together in such an intimate setting.

"Here's a question I would like to ask, but I don't want to offend you both," I piped up, gnawing on my lower lip.

"Shoot. We won't be offended," Zak assured. I glanced at Ronan, and he simply nodded. Both men were relaxed and happy, so I clutched my courage and asked.

"You two are really comfortable sharing a woman during sex. Have you two ever... I mean, have you ever experimented...

with each other?" I asked, my face warming.

Ronan bit back a smile and Zak grinned.

"Fair question," Ronan mumbled.

"Have you?" I asked, my heart beating fast. I wasn't sure I wanted to know.

"Would it disgust you if we had?" Ronan asked, watching me carefully. I ducked my head and forced my initial reaction out. It wasn't relevant here.

"Disgust probably isn't the right word. I've never really considered two men together until recently. I mean... I was brought up with my parents telling me it was the devil's work and abhorrent for two men to sleep together. But... I just never could think of it as such a vile thing," I answered honestly.

"Your parents are big on religion, huh?" Zak asked.

I scoffed and gave a little laugh. "Yeah, you could say that."

"Well... yes, we have," Ronan answered. I looked up at them both and Zak smiled, seeing my need for clarification.

"We've never kissed, and we've never fucked each other. But there's been times during sex where we've given a hand to the other... literally. We've both helped each other to come several times over the years, and I suspect we will do so many more times. Neither of us are attracted to men, but in the moment, when things are hot and heavy with a woman between us, it doesn't seem to bother either of us when we need the extra help," Zak explained.

"Oh," I answered, sitting on that for a moment. The guys gave me a little bit of time to think about that before Ronan tapped my thigh with his finger.

"Are you okay?" he asked.

"Yeah. Yes, I mean... of course. I was just... picturing it," I answered with a flush. Zak chuckled and Ronan smiled softly, but I caught the way his shoulders relaxed slightly.

"Do you think it's something you'd do in the future?" I asked.

"Fuck? Or continue to help when it's needed?" Ronan asked.

"Fuck," I answered quickly.

Ronan shook his head. "Like I said, we're not attracted to men, and so I don't ever see us fucking the other, and I'm not interested in sucking his cock, and I doubt Zak wants to suck mine," Ronan began.

"Not really," Zak added. I chuckled and Ronan smirked.

"What if a woman you're with wants you to do more? Would it be something you'd consider or is it an outright *no*?"

Ronan didn't answer right away, and I watched with interest as his gaze rose to meet Zak's. Both men stared at each other, a silent conversation passing between them.

"I guess... it would be something we'd have to decide if ever the request was made," Ronan answered slowly, still looking at his friend.

"I'm pretty open to a lot of things, but we'd have to consider what it would do to our friendship. It wouldn't just be a matter of being comfortable with sexual exploration," Zak added.

"I understand," I said with a small nod, feeling an odd tingle down low at the thought of the two of them together.

"But I won't say never to a helping hand in the future," Ronan added after a small silence.

"Do you feel the same way, Zak?" I asked.

He thought for a moment and nodded. "Yes."

I marveled at how easily they took my question and how they honestly thought about the question and their answers. Neither of them worried about seeming less masculine for even considering having sex with the other.

"Would you want us to keep doing it in the future if you were a part of it? Or would you prefer us to keep our hands for you alone?" Ronan asked.

I wanted to grin at the fact that he was even asking.

"Umm… I'm not sure," I answered honestly. "I mean… a part of me feels like if you were helping each other out, that if you had to look to each other to get what you needed…" I trailed off, my chest pricking at the memory of my fiancé.

"You'd feel like you weren't enough," Zak finished for me. I nodded and blinked quickly when my eyes stung.

"That fiancé and friend of yours sure did a number on you," Ronan whispered softly, his dark eyes looking at me with such intensity that I had to look away. Why did I feel like he saw through all my layers with that look?

~

The fifth morning included a similar wakeup, and I decided right then and there that every woman's life would be a lot better if they woke up to the kind of orgasms these men gave me.

This morning, I returned the favor, which resulted in me making Ronan come in my mouth. Zak then pulled me up onto my hands and knees and placed me over Ronan so I was straddling him. He then took his position behind me and fucked me on top of Ronan. I had never in my life imagined such a scenario. Being fucked by Zak while on Ronan's lap while he was fully clothed had been so hot, I had no gauge for it. But being fucked by Zak while straddling a naked and aroused Ronan was something else. Every thrust from Zak ground me down over Ronan's hardening cock, and I could feel both men between my thighs. Images of what we could be doing, what we might end up doing together in a similar scenario were bright and vivid in my mind, but the thoughts were driven out when I watched Ronan reach between my legs to stroke me, his hand moving further back to cup and fondle Zak's balls as he thrust into me. Zak gave a low groan of pleasure and I gasped, my sheath spasming around Zak at how forbidden and terribly hot that was. Ronan watched my face carefully, those dark eyes of his missing nothing.

He smiled, his eyes warming, and he leaned forward to suck at my nipples while he continued to stroke Zak.

It was all too much, and I came screaming for the second time that morning.

"Well…" Zak murmured sometime later, still braced over me as I lay flat on Ronan's chest, struggling to get my breath back. "I think it's safe to say you don't find Ronan and I giving each other the occasional assist a turn-off."

I laughed into Ronan's chest and shook my head.

"Not in the least. I didn't realize how hot I'd find that," I admitted, surprised.

Ronan kissed my head and Zak slowly pulled out of me and collapsed beside us on the bed.

The beautiful moment was broken when my stomach gave an embarrassingly loud rumble. We all laughed, and Zak leaned down to kiss me thoroughly before he sighed.

"I'm going to go start breakfast," Zak announced, kissing me quickly before he rolled from bed.

I watches Zak's naked butt head out the bedroom door with a stupid grin on my face before I turned to look at Ronan again who was watching me intently, curiously.

"What?"

"Are you okay this morning?" he asked, tracing a hand up my thigh.

"I'm good and happy," I answered with a laugh. His eyes searched my expression, and I felt a small blush heat my face, memories of last night coming back. The way I'd cried out, the things I'd said, the scene I went along with. Somehow, I could still feel every touch, stroke, and thrust. The words they said to me were still running through my mind, and I squeezed my thighs together in reaction. Ronan slowly grinned, a sexy, heated smile.

"I'm glad," he answered. "And how are you feeling about... about the scenes we've been playing?" he asked, sucking in a breath, his expression turning serious. I rolled slowly to my side to study his face, another memory floating back to me. They'd talked about someone else last night, someone who had called them monsters, accused them of rape and of being sick. He was really worried I'd do the same thing in the light of day.

Over the last few days we'd done a lot of different scenes, but the ones that seemed to make Ronan lose all control were the ones were I pleaded for him to stop, to let me go, to not fuck me. He was worried about how that made him look, about the kind of man that made him, and about how I would look at him.

"I think, as different as it was for me, it was hot. Despite how they played out, I liked doing things that made you happy, that brought you pleasure... I've never felt safer in my life," I replied honestly. Relief and doubt clashed in his eyes, and I reached out to trace his stubble-coated jaw.

"What are you so afraid of, Ronan? If I didn't like what happened, if you guys made me feel unsafe... do you really think I'd still be here?"

"I worry we frighten you too much to leave," he answered, voice husky.

"If that's what you really think... I'll go back to my room this morning. But when I come back on my own, you need to let down your wall. You asked me to trust you, to know that I can trust you, but you're the one not fully trusting me. And it's going to be too hard to keep opening up with you when you keep a wall between us," I replied.

He looked surprised, shocked, and a little ashamed.

"I... we have had bad experiences before," he explained.

I nodded and sighed. "Trust is a two-way street, Ronan. I trust you to touch me like you do, speak to me the way you do. I trust you to show me things about myself that I wouldn't have ever known on my own. I trusted you to tie me up, and let you and Zak use me like you did... and I knew you'd never hurt me intentionally. I had to trust that if I said the word, you'd stop. I need you to trust me when I say that I'm okay, and that I liked what we did. I'm not about to run from here screaming and telling people lies," I replied.

His eyes shuttered, but not before I caught the brief stab of pain. I wanted to be able to reach him, to give him some sort of assurance that I wasn't this woman who had hurt him in the past, but he wouldn't believe anything but my actions.

"I'm going to get up and have some breakfast. You can join us when you're ready," I said before I leaned forward to kiss him and got up. I didn't look back as I got off the bed and made my way on wobbly legs out of the bedroom. In the bathroom, I did my business and finger combed my hair into some semblance of order before I tied my hair back into a rough ponytail and entered the kitchen.

Zak already had eggs cooking and toast buttered, and I smiled. "I managed to walk into the bar of the only two men who are truly perfect, didn't I?"

Zak grinned and winked at me. I took a moment to look him over. He was bare except for the black briefs. His wide chest was impressive to watch, the muscles beneath the skin rippling seductively as he moved. I loved watching the tattoos on his skin and wondered if I'd ever be brave enough to get one.

"If you keep looking at me like that, baby girl, I'm going to have you for breakfast," Zak growled. I dragged my gaze back to his face and smiled.

"I might let you," I returned. He groaned and closed his eyes. Laughing, I slid up behind him and wrapped my arms around his waist, a little uncertain if this kind of intimacy was okay. It was funny, really, that I worried if wrapping my arms around him as he made breakfast was too intimate when he'd literally been inside me less than twelve hours ago, sharing me with another man. But intimacy was an odd thing, and it came in many forms. As close as we'd already been, doing things like this somehow seemed even more so.

He lifted an arm to press a couple of buttons on his phone and then the kitchen was filled with music. Zak took my hand and stepped sideways, spinning me into his arms. I inhaled sharply and laughed, and he grinned down at me. Goddamn, this man was gorgeous.

"Dance with me, Hazel," he urged, pulling me in close as he swayed us around the kitchen. It would have been impossible to wipe the smile from my face even had I wanted to.

"What about breakfast?" I asked, laughing when he dipped me backwards.

"I thought I got to eat you?" he answered, waggling his eyebrows. Beaming, I shook my head at his teasing. After a few more seconds he spun me out again.

"You could tempt me to stay forever with suggestions like that," I joked.

Zak groaned and pulled me in tight for a moment, brushing his thumb over my cheek. "Don't say that. We want to give you some time before we... well, before we talk about more," he added, ducking his head.

I wanted to ask what he meant by that, but Ronan came in then, and the mood shifted. Not a lot, but the playfulness in Zak seemed to have lessened and he gave me a quick kiss before going back to making breakfast.

We sat at the small table an hour later, fed and full, the kitchen clean after a joint effort. I kept noticing the unspoken conversation between Ronan and Zak as they finished drying and putting away the dishes and decided that it was time I be let in on the problem.

"What's going on?" I asked as I let out the sink and dried my hands with the hand towel. The guys looked between each other again and Zak sighed, almost like he was unsure how to approach the subject.

"We weren't sure what your plans are now. Are you going back home today? Or are you intending to stay a little longer?" he asked, not looking at me as he spoke.

I didn't want to answer because I didn't want to think. I wanted to go a little longer without considering my life back home.

"I haven't given it much thought," I answered softly.

"Maybe you should," Ronan interrupted. My eyes snapped to Ronan, and Zak kept his arms around me. "Maybe you should give your next step some thought," he clarified.

Sorrow began to weigh down on me, and I ducked my head again. Since I'd started sleeping with them, Ronan kept asking me what my plans are for the future in one way or another. Why did it feel like he was trying to shove me out the door? I frowned down at my feet, and he stepped in closer.

"And if I don't want to think about it right now?"

There was a small silence and then Ronan cleared his throat. Zak had gone stiff, and when I raised my gaze to look at these two incredible men, I saw that his jaw was tight, and his eyes were burning at his friend. They were having another silent argument; one I was not privy to.

"I think it's best for us all if you take some time to consider where you're going next or what you're going to do with your life now. I mean, you still have to talk to your fiancé, correct? Are you even still engaged? Have you spoken to him since you saw him in bed with your friend?" Ronan asked. These were all fair questions, but I hated them.

"No," I murmured.

"You can't make a decision until you've had that conversation," Ronan continued. I concentrated on my breathing, feeling my anger begin to rise and my cheeks heat. I was not ready to do that. I'd spent my entire life listening to people tell me what they thought I should and should not do. I didn't need it from Ronan, not now, not when I needed to bury my head in the sand a little longer and just continue to explore this possible new me.

"And what decision is there to make, Ronan? Are you offering more than just a couple of nights of hot sex?" I demanded.

"Are you *wanting* more than a few nights of hot sex?" he threw back stubbornly.

I shook my head. "That's not fair, and it's not what I asked." Ronan took a moment to think before he took a half step back, leaning his hip on the counter, his arms crossed over his chest. He looked deceptively lazy, but the tension in his shoulders and jaw gave him away.

"I'm not saying this to hurt you or upset you. Obviously, we don't want you to go, I just want you to really think about things," Ronan continued.

"I get it," I snapped, pulling away from Zak. He tried to hold onto me, like he didn't want me to leave.

"No, I don't think you do," Ronan argued, straightening to step in close to me. He tilted my head back and I glared up at him, his dark eyes frustrated, dominating.

"You want me to leave, Ronan. It's why you're pushing me away; it's why you won't let me close. And I get it, I'm a temporary fuck for you before you move onto the next girl, but at least have the balls to say it instead of dressing your reasons up as if they're meant to be what's best for me."

He blinked, his eyes widened, and he was momentarily

speechless. "Now, wait just a minute—"

"Let me go," I said lowly, trying to pull away when he gripped my upper arms.

"Hazel, listen—"

"I said, let me go, Ronan," I repeated, my voice louder this time.

"Haz—"

"Vanilla!"

He froze, his face paling and his grip on my arms dropping immediately.

Zak looked at us, his eyes wide in shock. I was breathing hard, upset, hurt, exhausted, and so damn confused. What the hell had happened to our beautiful morning? We were having such a great day. Why was I so hurt? Everything Ronan had said was true. I needed to take some time to really consider things. A part of me was upset that he wasn't being all that honest with himself, that he was using my issues as a buffer between us and a reason to keep me at arm's length. But why did hearing him say any of it hurt so much?

"I'm sorry... you're right. I should go," I whispered, brushing past them both. Neither of them followed me and I grabbed my shoes, my bag, and dress, and hurried for the front door.

"Hazel," Zak called, and I froze, turning back to look at him.

"I'm really sorry, Zak. Ronan is right. Maybe this is just too much for me. Maybe I'm just confused," I whispered, my vision blurring with tears.

"I don't believe it. You felt it. You felt what this is, I know you did," he told me, stepping closer.

I held up a hand to ward him off and he stopped, his eyes pained, and I hated that I was the one to put that there.

"I need to go," I whispered brokenly. His words were ones I wanted desperately to hear, but they were a dagger to my heart right now. A part of me knew it was too soon, that what I was feeling was too much too soon. And another part of me wondered if it was all just temporary anyway.

With one last pained look, I hurried out of the apartment and raced down the stairs. Fumbling with the locks on the bar door for a moment, I threw them open and stepped outside. I hurried down the stairs and was safely ensconced in my room in record time. I leaned back against the door, breathing heavily, my things still clutched in my hands. Then, I slowly slid to the floor and burst into tears.

CHAPTER FOURTEEN

I had been sitting on the floor for far too long. My legs were stiff, my back ached, and my face was swollen from crying. Mostly, I was mad at myself.

My whole life I'd been told what to do, how to dress, what to think, say, and believe. Every part of my life had been planned out for me by the time I was ten, and I had gone along with it all. I'd let myself become brainwashed into thinking my contribution to society revolved around my abilities to snag a rich husband, produce beautiful children, and to arrange flowers artfully while handling the household staff.

Walking in on Richard cheating on me... it had hurt. I was still trying to figure out if it was my heart that was broken, or my pride. When I was with Richard, I'd often wondered if what I felt for him was love, and if it was, then all the romance books and movies were lying. We weren't passionate and hot, and my heart didn't thud faster when he walked into a room, not since the first few months we'd been dating. But I was definitely embarrassed that they'd been fooling around on me, and I hadn't even suspected it. The betrayal stung and the humiliation at having the wool pulled over my eyes had been devastating. After having some space from it, however, I now realized it was the best thing that could have happened to me. It made me look at my life, *really* look at it, and see where I was headed. Maybe I wasn't super intelligent, but I was smart, and I'd never been brave enough to look at my life carefully before, but that was all in the past. Now, I knew there was more, and I was beginning to see that I was worth more than being an accessory on my husband's arm. I knew I was capable of more than smiling prettily and caring for a man.

Ronan had been right.

It was time for me to stop burying my head in the sand and start facing facts. Only then could I make an informed decision about my life and where I wanted it to go from here.

I didn't love Rich, not really. I loved the idea of him. He had fit the description of the kind of man I was supposed to end up with perfectly, on paper at least. But I didn't love him.

And he didn't love me.

Zak and Ronan had managed to make me feel more for them in just two days than my fiancé had in years. How?

"You felt it. You felt what this is, I know you did."

Zak's voice rang in my head, and I exhaled slowly. I did feel it... whatever it was. It was intense and incredible, and it was something that required someone to be onboard with one hundred percent. Did I want that? Was the new direction of my life going to be decided by my love life?

No.

But maybe it could help to shape it.

So where did that leave me? I knew I wasn't going back to Richard, but was I going back home? Was there any point? I could use this as an excuse to set out on my own and live a little. Twisting my lips in thought, I shook my head. What would I do here in the meantime? I had enough money on my cards to keep me here for a while—I groaned. I'd have to stop using my cards. Rich was a lawyer, and he had connections. He could find out where my last transaction had been made and find me. I had used my card at the gas station and paid in cash at the motel—that had been a safety issue on my part. I'd used a fake name and paid in cash because I hadn't wanted anyone here to know who I was or have my information. This place wasn't exactly fancy, and I was alone. So, at the moment, Rich would know I went to the gas station. Hopefully he'd think I just kept on driving.

I could deal with all that later.

But was I *ever* going to go back home? Afterall, what was there waiting for me but two parents who were distant in their affection and a whole heap of racism and sexism? I couldn't go back to being the woman I was before; it was impossible. I had broken free of the mold they had so carefully shaped me from, and there was no putting me back.

I could start over with the single bag of clothing I'd brought and the money in my bank, nothing else back home meant anything to me, and I already knew my parents would *never* change their beliefs and way of thinking to ever accept the life I wanted now. I had my car, my wits, and my wallet… I'd make do.

I looked around the room and nodded. Okay, I'd start by doing a little shopping. Then I was going to come back and call Rich and my parents to let them know I was okay, but that I wasn't coming back.

"Get up, Hazel. Your life is waiting for you," I whispered to myself.

~

"You're the girl from the bar."

I'd taken a drive to the nearest second-hand store and had filled up a basket with some new-to-me clothes and shoes—stuff that felt more like *me*.

I turned with a frown at the voice behind me. A stunning woman stood there. She was about five-foot-seven, with bright blue eyes and mahogany brown hair—a knockout if I ever saw one—and she was currently looking me over with curious eyes.

"Sorry?"

"You're the girl from the bar. The one Ronan and Zak were

dancing with," she expanded.

"Uh..." I trailed off, not knowing how to continue this conversation. Her face broke into a grin, and she gave me a mischievous look and a wink.

"Don't worry; everyone in this town knows Zak and Ronan like to share. None of us know why, but none of us really care, either. It's just how they've always been. No one judges them, and they're really good about not judging the rest of us," she continued brightly.

I blinked several times, wishing my mind would hurry up and catch up.

"Steph, shut up. You've stunned her," another gorgeous woman reprimanded, coming to stand beside the first. She was roughly the same size with fluffy blonde hair that gave her the appearance of a few extra inches in height. Cherry brown eyes shone back at me, and I noticed the gentle smattering of freckles across her nose and engaging smile.

"Oh, sorry!" the one named Steph said, looking abashed. "I sometimes say things without thinking. I just wanted to say hi and see what kind of person you are. It's not just anyone who gains the attention of those men, and the last one was such a disaster we weren't sure they'd be open to it again," Steph continued.

"The last one?" I murmured, shaking off my initial shock. Both women looked at each other and pulled a face.

"Taylor," they said together. Ah, the infamous Taylor.

"She's the one who accused them of assault?" I asked, tossing it out there.

"She said a *lot* about them, to anyone who would listen," the blonde one answered dispassionately.

A bad taste layered my tongue, and I shifted my basket.

"They loved her?" I asked.

Steph shrugged.

"They cared about her, I guess. But she wasn't here long and wouldn't keep her mouth shut about their activities in the bedroom. Eventually both guys got questioned by the cops, but nothing stuck. Still, rumors never die, and neither of them have been very open about things since. They don't hook up with women who walk into the bar anyway," the blonde one answered.

"Sorry, I am being really rude. I'm Jessie, and this is my wife, Stephanie. We own the hair and beauty salon in town," she explained, holding out her beautifully manicured nails. I smiled and shook it. There was just something about these women that reached me. I liked their energy.

"Hazel," I answered.

"Oh wow, pretty name," Steph complimented. I smiled shyly and she grinned, then looked down at my basket with a raised eyebrow.

"Are you intending to stay a while? You didn't look like you were from around here, and we figured you were just in town for the weekend," Jessie asked.

I shrugged. "I'm, uh… I'm kind of trying to figure some things in my life out. So, for now, I'm here, but I don't know what that means," I answered. Jessie blinked at me and then turned to Steph before both women turned back to me with soft smiles.

"Do you want to get a coffee, darl? The salon is closed today, and we'd be happy to sit down and chat with you," Jessie offered. I opened my mouth to say no; after all, I didn't know these women. But I liked them. I felt like they were genuine people, and Christ, did I need to speak to someone. I needed girl-talk.

"Look, you don't have to tell us anything if you don't want to, but I'm a hairdresser, which pretty much means I'm a therapist, except that I make you look gorgeous when you leave," Jessie explained with a smile. I laughed and her pretty eyes sparkled.

"Steph is a nail technician, and that makes her one too. There aren't a lot of people in this town, so we all kind of get to know each other one way or another. And like I said, none of us have seen the guys look at a woman like they have with you the last two nights. If you're here and planning to stay a while, we'd love to get to know you. Maybe we can offer you some advice?" Jessie continued.

My eyes stung again, and I blinked and glanced down at my basket, then nodded.

"You know, I think I'd like that. But let me buy the coffee," I suggested.

"Oh wow, you just got bumped into my top ten favorite people," Steph returned. I grinned and followed the women to the counter where I paid for my clothing and then out of the shop. A few minutes later, we were ensconced in a little booth in the back of a café, giving us some privacy.

"Okay, first, I gotta know... how the hell does a tiny thing like you take two massive men like Ronan and Zak? I mean, we've all seen the outline of their bodies at one point or another, and neither of them are what you'd class as small... or even average. They're definitely on the extra-large scale, and you're so tiny!" Steph cried.

I felt my eyes widen in shock and Jessie slapped her wife's arm with a frown.

"You can't just ask her something like that right off the bat," she scolded.

"I was just curious. I mean, those are seriously *hot* males, and I am not the only woman who has noticed, nor the only one who will be a little jealous of the attention you'll be getting from them," she added. I frowned and looked from Steph to her wife and back.

"Steph swings both ways, but she settled for me two years ago,"

Jessie answered, obviously seeing my confusion.

"Oh," I whispered with a smile.

"I didn't *settle* for you, baby. You swept me away and won my heart. There is a difference," Steph corrected. Jessie beamed as I watched with fascination and a little awe at the utter adoration and love on their faces for one another. Jessie kissed Steph, and it wasn't exactly chaste either.

"Okay, so let's start with where you're from, Hazel," Jessie said with a grin. I huffed out a breath, and then consequences be damned, spilled my whole, sordid tale.

In return, they'd told me about Taylor and what she'd done to my guys. And yes, that was what I was calling them, because I felt strangely protective and territorial over them. Taylor had been a visitor to this town many times over the years, traveling through for some sort of work—they didn't tell me what. She stayed here every other weekend and spent time with the guys. Steph understood the relationship to be exclusive—the guys and Taylor. Apparently, they were half-way in love with her when they realized she was running her mouth to the entire town. When the guys got mad at her for spilling bedroom secrets, she got defensive and mad and started acting scared. It got to the point where she ran to the cops and told them that Ronan didn't listen to her when she told him to stop, that he forced himself on her and Zak held her down for him. My mind flashed to our roleplay the other night, but even now, I couldn't see them as rapists.

Jessie asked me if I was staying with the guys, but I wasn't sure. I hadn't had much of a chance to get to know them, but maybe I could make time. Maybe we could all take some time to talk and see if this chemistry between us extended outside the bedroom. I sighed. This at least explained Zak's hurt and Ronan's hesitation

and guard when it came to me. He wasn't willing to get hurt
again.

~

Three hours later, I was back in my motel room and exhausted,
but my mind wouldn't stop running.

Ronan and Zak liked to play rough in the bedroom and let a
fantasy come alive with a willing partner who played along, but
they would never hurt someone. The guys had been very clear
with me about what I needed to say and to *never* go ahead with a
scenario I was not comfortable with. They had been almost
annoying in their attempts to make me understand.

Now I knew why.

Jessie and Steph were fun and intelligent, and they'd given me
advice on how to proceed, and I was pretty sure I was going to
take it.

I pulled on a pair of faded jeans and a white peasant blouse I'd
bought from the store and put my hair up into a ponytail.
Already, I felt more like myself and not like the doll I'd been
pretending to be for so long.

First thing first, I wanted to call home. I had to speak to my
parents, and I needed to talk to Rich. Once that was done, I
wanted to go speak to the guys and apologize. Ronan had been
right this morning, and I'd run off because I hadn't wanted to
hear it. But that was the act of a child, and I was not a spoiled
brat. I was a woman on a mission to claim ownership of her own
life, and I couldn't run away from truths anymore, no matter
how harsh they were. I still thought I was right in my assessment
of Ronan, though. He had been pushing me away because he
didn't want to open himself up to trusting me. Heck, maybe
Ronan and Zak wouldn't be a part of my future, maybe they
were just there to help me get to the next stage. But no matter

what, they still deserved an apology. My heart sank a little at the idea of not being with them in the future, but I couldn't let myself get wrapped up in what they made me feel. I couldn't make a decision about the direction of my life by basing it on a *possible* relationship.

I sucked in a deep breath and snatched up my phone. I ignored the notifications and called Rich without giving myself any time to think.

"Hazel!" he shouted in relief.

"Hi, Richard," I greeted, closing my eyes on the sound of his voice.

"Where the hell are you? Where have you been? Are you okay? You haven't spoken to anyone and we're all worried sick. You just ran off and no one knows where you are or when you're coming back. Your parents are going out of their minds, your friends are worried, *I* am worried," he said in a rush, barely taking a second to breathe.

"Rich, stop. Just stop," I whispered, blinking back the tears.

"Hazel——" he whispered, his voice laden with sadness and regret.

"No, you don't get to speak to me like that," I snapped, stiffening my spine. "I am just calling to let you know, in case it wasn't plainly obvious already, that we aren't getting married anymore. I'm not coming home, either. I've decided my life is better lived away from that town and the things they believe and practice. I never truly fit in there anyway, and now I have the perfect chance to leave it all behind for good," I said quickly, proud when my voice came out steady.

"Hazel——" he started again, but I cut him off.

"No, Rich. I'm not going back. I just want to know… how long were you two—how long did you…" I trailed off, my voice breaking and my heart twisting at the pain they put me through. There was a small silence as he tried to think. "Just tell me, Rich.

You both owe me that much."

"Three years," he answered, and I hated that I could hear the regret in his voice. I closed my eyes on the dagger in my chest and couldn't hold back the sob.

"Hazel, I'm so sor—"

"No!" I shouted. "You don't get to apologize, Rich. Neither of you do. You made a fool out of me. You went behind my back for three years! God, how stupid was I? I bet you both got a good laugh out of that," I snapped, wiping away the tears on my cheeks.

"It wasn't like that, Hazel. You have to know we both love you," Richard said hurriedly.

"That is not love, Rich. Not on the behalf of a fiancé nor a friend. I can't do this right now, but I just needed to let you know this is over," I snipped, taking in an unsteady breath.

"I have no right to ask, Hazel, I know I don't, but are you going to... have you told anyone?" he asked, his voice small. Outrage filled me at the question, and I wanted to hurl my phone at the wall.

"*That's* what you're worried about? Your reputation?"

"Hazel—"

"Fuck you, Richard. Have a nice life," I seethed and ended the call. I clenched the phone in my hand tightly, struggling to get my blood pressure down and to blink away the tears. He was worried about people knowing what he'd done. He didn't want it getting back to his bosses that he wasn't really a family man. He wanted to keep his good standing in our town and not be known as an adulterer...

I shook my head.

It was painful, but it was good that this happened, and in the end, far better than the life I would have lived had we gotten married and he continued to cheat on me.

I glanced down at my phone again, knowing I needed to make at least one last phone call today. Refusing to give myself time to chicken out, I dialed.

"Hazel? Baby?"

"Hi, Momma," I greeted softly, blinking back the tears at the sound of her voice. She may be materialistic, and we may not have the same values, but she was still my momma.

"Oh, baby, where are you? Where did you go? Why did you go? We've all been worried sick about you," she cried, and I wanted to smile at the hysteria in her voice. I loved my mother, but the woman was prone to dramatics at the drop of a hat. Hearing her cry out so hysterically was almost comforting.

"I'm fine, Momma, really. But I, uh... Rich and I... we're not getting married anymore," I told her.

Silence.

"He broke up with you?" she breathed in disbelief.

"No," I mumbled.

"What did you do, sugar?" she asked. I frowned and blinked confusedly, shaking my head.

"I'm sorry—what did *I* do?" I repeated.

"We all know that man is crazy about you. So, you had to have done *something* for him to want to end things."

"I just told you he didn't break up with me, Momma. I broke up with *him,*" I clarified. She made a *tsk*ing sound and I could practically see her shaking her head.

"I'm sure if you apologize for whatever you did, Hazel, he'll take you back. Richard is a good man with a well-paying job. He comes from a respectable family, and I don't need to tell you how hard it is to find one nowadays. You really shouldn't be out there on our own."

"It's not 1901 anymore, Momma. Women can be out in the world without a chaperone."

"Hazel-Maree, you watch your tone with me, young lady. Now tell me where you are and your daddy can come get you," she snapped in that waspish tone only a mother could use. I shook my head and drew in a shaky breath.

"No, Momma. I'm not coming home. I don't want to live there anymore."

"Hazel, you don't know what you're sayin', baby," my mother whispered, sounding faint.

"I do, Momma. I can't live like that anymore. I'm not coming home. I love you, and I love Daddy, but I can't pretend to be someone I'm not another day, and I'm not marrying Richard," I added. There was silence and I forced my emotions under control.

"I love you, and I will call you next week. If you don't want to talk to me, I'll understand. But this is happening, and this is how I feel. I love you, Momma. Kiss Daddy for me," I whispered and ended the call before switching it off.

Closing my eyes, I fell backwards onto the bed and dragged in deep breath after deep breath, desperate to calm myself down. I felt like I'd just thrown myself off a cliff without a parachute, and I was trying to find a ledge to hold onto.

CHAPTER FIFTEEN

I spent the afternoon lying on my bed and wondering what I was going to do now. I waited for the regret to settle in; the feeling that I had made a mistake calling things off with Richard and that I needed my parents.

But to my surprise, it never came.

Instead, I was mad.

I was mad at my parents for bringing me up in a community like the one they had. I was mad at my best friend for betraying me; the one person I should have been able to go to and talk to about anything, trust with anything. I was mad at Richard for lying to me for so long, for going behind my back, for making me feel like shit... and for giving me four years' worth of shitty sex! Mostly though, I was mad at myself.

I'd allowed myself to be lulled into complacency there, had let myself off the hook from being someone better because "this is how my parents brought me up."

No.

Maybe I couldn't help what family I was born into or where I had grown up, but I was a grown ass adult, and there wasn't a damn person I could blame for my life right now but myself.

I needed to make changes.

I was free now, out from under my parents' rule and their beliefs. It hurt to know they would likely never come around, and that by choosing this life for myself, I was choosing a life without them, but I couldn't control their actions, only my own. I'd always known there was more out there, and that the beliefs they'd been shoving down my throat from a young age were not necessarily mine.

At the end of the day, all I could think was there was no point in doing something I loved with my life if there was no one I cared about at my side. I wanted people I loved, cared about, and that I considered friends. And right as I ran away from my old life, I'd managed to find something just like that here in this tiny town full of strange people. Well, strange for me.

Thinking about Zak and Ronan left me with a deep yearning to see them and be with them. I knew it wasn't smart to base my future on two men I barely knew, but some part of me *did* know them. Some part of me understood them on a level that required no words.

Remembering our time together, hearing their voices in my ear, and thinking about the morning we'd spend together just talking and laughing... I'd never felt more comfortable with anyone else in my life. They weren't just great in bed—that was a gross understatement—they were also kind, caring, and considerate. Both were honest and warm, and they seemed to care about me. Knowing all of that was what brought me to the bar door that evening as the sun was going down. The closed sign was still up, so I had to assume they weren't open tonight for dinner. I'd spent the day away from them and their roaming hands. I'd gotten perspective, I'd talked to other people, and I had made it clear to those back home that I was not coming back and that my wedding was off. This was a new start for me—a possible new life. Now I just had to be brave enough to take it.

I bit my lower lip and carefully tried the bar door. It was still unlocked, and I entered, not sure if I'd be welcome.

The room was dim, but there were a few lights on which told me they'd been down here at some point. Quiet music played on the overhead speakers, filling the room with comforting noise. I'd taken three steps inside when Zak came out from the storage room, a large box on his shoulder. He paused when he saw me, joy briefly lit his eyes followed closely by wariness and concern.

"Hazel," he said my name softly, carefully, putting the heavy box on the bar.

"Hey," I whispered, clearing my throat as I took another step forward. Zak's gaze ran over me from head to toe and back, a small smile twisting his lips.

"I went shopping," I explained, knowing he was noting my change in outfits.

"It suits you," he admitted.

Silence followed and I struggled to find the right words.

"Is everything okay?" he asked, stepping forward before seeming to catch himself. He stopped a good twelve feet away, and I despised every inch of distance.

"I... I need to apologize about this morning. I was feeling attacked, but nothing Ronan said was wrong. I... I'm sorry," I said quickly, my breath hitching.

"He was wrong to push you when you weren't ready," Zak defended.

I shrugged. "I can't keep blaming everyone else for the way my life turns out. It's time to start taking a stand, and I couldn't do that when I refused to face the issues I had."

"Had?" Zak asked, noting my use of the past tense.

I nodded. "I called Rich today, my *ex*-fiancé. He's very clear on the fact that we're over. I also called my mother... she was less than pleased with the news."

"So, what are you going to do?" he asked, stepping a little closer.

I shrugged. "I don't know, exactly, but I'm not going home to my parents. I can't go back there. There are too many things that limit me, and I've had enough."

Hope brightened Zak's eyes, and he inched closer again. "Are you moving on from here?"

"I have no immediate plans. I'm a little lost, honestly. I'm trying to find my next step, trying to figure out what I need to do next. But right now, I don't want to look beyond where I am," I answered, my heart thudding as I watched those amazing eyes take all of me in. It was crazy how right it felt to be in this bar, in Zak's presence, and feel like this was exactly where I was meant to be. Was it really so simple? Could I really have run straight from one relationship and found myself in the one I was meant to be in all along?

"You came back."

I turned to see Ronan on the bottom step of the staircase that led to the apartment, his dark gaze locked on me.

"I told you I wasn't scared of you."

"Ronan—" Zak started warningly.

"I heard what she said. I was on the stairs," Ronan cut in.

I looked between both men and frowned. "Everything alright between you two?"

Zak shrugged. "I got mad at him for scaring you off because I didn't want you to leave. Just because he was feeling vulnerable and scared shouldn't mean I miss out on the girl too."

"He's been mad at me all day, tore me a new one for causing you to leave this morning," Ronan added with a small shrug, his eyes never leaving my face.

"I'm sorry. I never wanted to be a point of contention between the two of you," I replied sadly.

Ronan shook his head and Zak stepped in close to me.

"It wasn't your fault. Ronan and I know what we want in a relationship, and we know who we are. We know whoever we end up with will have to be a woman we both want and who wants us. I... I like you, a lot. And I wanted to see where things would go with you. I wanted to persuade you to stay. But Ronan was right, I was taking advantage of your vulnerability, and it wouldn't have been fair," Zak explained.

I ducked my head, my cheeks warming. "And now?"

"That depends on you," Ronan answered.

"Does it?" I fired back. He frowned and I sighed, taking a step back and running my hands over my head.

"Look... I didn't come to this town looking to start anything. I literally ran away from a bad relationship and ended up in your bed. I wasn't prepared for that. And while it seems really soon to consider anything real, I know I wasn't in love with Rich, so my heart isn't in need of healing, not where he's concerned," I began.

"What are you saying?" Zak asked, looking almost afraid to ask.

"I really like the two of you. I don't know what either of you are looking for, but I feel like... I feel like we have something. More than just amazing chemistry in bed, I mean. This could be... something, if we let it," I began, quickly scanning their faces as I spoke to see if anything I said caused them to clam up. Neither one of their expressions changed, and so I pushed on.

"You both have an idea of how I lived before. You know things outside of the boring and beige are very odd for me, so I'm a little out of my depth here. I am also a little lost right now for direction. I don't know what I want to do or where I want to go, but I do know that I will regret not coming here and seeing if you two are open to exploring... whatever this is.," I continued, stumbling over my words and messing the whole thing up.

Silence met my declaration and I steeled myself for rejection. Could Jessie and Steph have misinterpreted things? Had I? Heat began to steal up my face and I was aware of my breathing escalating out of nerves.

"To make things clear, you want to try a relationship... with us both?" Zak asked.

"Well, I assumed you were a package deal," I quipped, twisting my fingers.

"And if we weren't?" Ronan asked. I tried not to show the hurt I felt, but judging from Zak's dark look at his friend, I hadn't been successful.

"I like you both, equally. But I can't imagine having one of you without the other," I answered softly. And it was true. I liked Zak, and I liked Ronan. Both of them for totally different reasons, and it seemed incomplete to have one and not the other. "Unless you two don't want me. That would be another problem altogether, but one I can easily correct by leaving," I added, doubt stabbing at me. It was very possible these two didn't want me. I was still new to all this, and I felt like maybe I wasn't experienced enough; I wasn't enough of a challenge for them to want me long-term. Crap... I hadn't thought much about that until now.

"That's not the issue here," Zak began, but Ronan cut in before he could continue.

"People like to talk."

I smiled gently at Zak who looked like he wanted to slap his friend, and I turned to Ronan who's dark eyes had never once left my face. It almost felt like he was testing me.

I shrugged. "If there's something I've learned growing up with people who constantly think they are above others, it's that people will talk no matter what. Let them talk."

"From what you've said, your parents will never approve of this. You could lose them," he continued, stepping in closer.

I laughed, but the sound was bitter. "At this point, it's not a matter of if I lose them or not, it's if *they* lose *me*. And they wouldn't approve of us for a lot of reasons, but none of them matter to me."

Silence.

"I need something from you, Ronan," I added. Zak frowned and Ronan's face turned stony.

"What?" Zak asked when his friend remained silent.

"I need *your* trust. You asked it of me, and I gave it, but I need you to stop guarding yourself, stop blocking me. That starts with telling me about Taylor and how badly she hurt you," I added. Both of them looked shocked at hearing her name and I breathed out slowly to steady myself.

"I ran into a couple of ladies today and we got talking. They explained how things looked from the outside to them, but aside from that, last night, I heard you both talking about what she accused you of and how she hurt you," I explained. Neither of them looked very happy, so I pushed on.

"I know you both have reasons to distrust this, but I am not her. I want to see where this goes, and that doesn't mean I am promising forever or even suggesting it, but it is a promise that I will try, and I will be open with you. For this to work, though, I need you guys to promise the same to me," I added.

More silence.

I waited for ten seconds, and then twenty that stretched into thirty before I sighed and nodded.

"Okay. Look… I didn't want to push you. I just… I would have hated myself if I didn't at least try," I murmured before I turned around and headed for the door.

"Wait!" Ronan called and I turned in time for him to reach me, tugging my hand. I looked up into his large, questioning eyes and he frowned.

"You know about Taylor?" he asked.

"I know what others have told me and what I heard you saying. I know she accused you of some awful things, that she tried to get you in trouble. I know that her bitterness at being reprimanded and dumped for sharing personal details about the two of you

with others made her try to get you both run out of town," I
explained. He shook his head, stunned.

"I want to see whatever this is between us. I don't care what
other people think, and I'm not worried about losing what I had
when it's not what I really wanted anyway. I do know that when I
think about walking away from the two of you, it hurts more
than it should, considering how little time we've known each
other," I explained honestly. Ronan remained silent and I moved
to the side to look at Zak.

"Zak, any follow up questions?" I asked. He grinned and shook his
head. "Then would one of you kiss me already? It feels like
forever since you've touched me."

Zak grinned and swooped me up, his mouth descending on mine,
and for the first time since I'd left the bar this morning, I felt
whole.

I wrapped my legs around his waist as he kissed me, long and
deep and sure, his hands on my back and my hands in his thick
hair. When we pulled apart, it was for Zak to pass me over to
Ronan. I wrapped my legs around him, but I didn't kiss him right
away. His dark eyes were still studying me, still searching.

"I'm here, Ronan. I'm not her, I will *never* be her. Please... will
you trust me?"

"You came back. I didn't think we'd see you again. I came to
your room this morning and your car was gone and no one
answered. I thought..." he trailed off, upset.

I shook my head. "I was just getting some things to start my new
life, but I couldn't have left things between us like that," I
promised. His eyes shone with appreciation, and I sighed when
he finally leaned in and kissed me. I clung to him, holding him
close, loving the way he kissed me, his tongue brushing mine, his
strong hands spreading wide over my back.

I was where I was meant to be... I was sure of it.

I was happy in this town where I could go to sleep in their arms, in their bed... between them both.

On and on the kiss went, and I hardly noticed we were moving until he sat me down. I broke away and looked down to see I was on the edge of a pool table. I grinned, and when he saw me smiling, he mirrored it, a happiness in his eyes I wasn't sure I'd see again.

"Lie back," he commanded, and I did so immediately. Ronan got to work pulling off my jeans and boots, and Zak locked the bar door. Quickly, both men yanked down the flies of their jeans and I felt my body respond drastically.

God, *yes*.

I pushed myself up onto my elbows and watched as Ronan yanked off my underwear, his large hands skimming my thighs up to my pussy. I moaned and he slid in one finger and then a second, his gaze jumping back to my face to watch me.

"Hazel—"

"I know the word to stop, Ronan," I gasped, leaning forward to frame his face with my hands. "Now hurry up and fuck me."

A devastating grin broke over his face and before I knew it, he'd yanked me to the edge of the pool table and thrust inside me. I opened my mouth to scream, both pleasure and pain coming over me, when a hand slapped over my mouth. I glanced up to see Zak behind me. Ronan had me so distracted I hadn't heard Zak or felt him climb onto the table, but he was there, his knees sliding under my neck keeping me propped up, his hand over my mouth and his eyes burning.

"Shh, baby girl," he whispered thickly. I moaned and Ronan thrust harder into me, over and over until he was fully inside me. He grunted in pleasure; his teeth gritted as he tried to hold on. It felt so good, so fucking good.

Zak's hands slid down to my top and he yanked the low scoop-neck down, pulling my breast out of my bra to play with the nipple. I moaned again, rocking against Ronan's hips, arching into Zak's hands.

"Good girl, Hazel," Ronan groaned. Yes, yes, *yes!* "This is gonna be hard and fast baby, no playing," he added. Good, I didn't need long and slow this time. I wanted both my guys, and I wanted them now. Ronan gritted his teeth and started slamming into me in earnest, his fingers playing with my clit, dragging me closer and closer to a screaming orgasm.

"Yes, Hazel. Come on my dick, baby. I can feel you getting close. Give it to me, sweetheart," Ronan groaned, the tendons on his neck standing out he strained against me. God, the man was beautiful. Zak pinched my nipple and I moaned, my eyes rolling back. I still couldn't scream, my moans muffled by the hand on my mouth. Shit, when had this kind of sex become so damn hot to me? Ronan ground against me, his fingers strumming my clit expertly as Zak's hands stroked my breasts. It was all too much…

"Yes!" I screamed beneath his hand and Ronan roared his release, shaking and coming hard inside me. I moaned; my legs wrapped tightly around him. I felt him come, felt his hot seed and I moaned again, something about it hotter than I ever—oh *shit*. I shook my head and tried to shout *vanilla*, but the hand over my mouth stopped me. Zak frowned down at me.

"Are you saying *vanilla?*" he asked.

I nodded. Immediately Zak yanked away his hand as if I'd burnt him and Ronan froze. He made to pull out, but I wrapped my legs around him.

"Wait, no, don't move," I gasped and panted. "I don't want to stop, I don't. I just, umm… you're not wearing a condom," I panted. Both men froze and then looked down to where Ronan's cock was already spent inside me.

"Shit," he breathed shakily. "I've never forgotten to suit up before."

"Me either," Zak gaped, stunned.

Silence fell as our minds raced over the implications.

"Okay, I'll go first. I'm clean, I've only ever been with one man. I mean, I didn't get tested again after I knew he cheated on me, but since it was my best friend, I'm fairly confident there were no STDs. I'm also on birth control, so we don't have to worry about accidentally creating a baby," I added.

Ronan swallowed hard, his gaze never wavering from where we were connected, and I looked from Zak and then back.

"Shit, I'm sorry. I even didn't think about a condom, I just wanted you so badly," I added, wondering if he was regretting this. I mean, there was no way for us to actually know if I had anything. I was certain I didn't, but there was still a possibility they couldn't ignore.

Ronan's dark gaze dragged to my face, and slid down to where we were connected again, his jaw tense. Shit.

"Ronan—"

"My cum is inside you right now, sweetheart, give me a damn second. This is so fucking hot, more than I ever thought it would be," he groaned, his voice gravelly and uneven. I froze. What? He withdrew slightly and thrust forward again, his eyes closing in pleasure.

"Ronan?" I breathed.

"I feel like I just claimed you, Hazel. *Fuck.*"

My breath was still shallow and choppy, and the way he was looking at me, the words he was saying, only made me that much hotter.

"My cum is inside your pussy. I just came inside you without a goddamn condom. Shit, it's almost enough to make me want to come again," he grunted, thrusting forward again, his eyes opening to reveal that dark, sinful stare. "I don't believe you have anything, Hazel. I just... I've never come inside a woman before, not without a condom. It's fucking hot," he whispered, his voice still uneven. I smiled and clenched tightly around him, and he swore under his breath. "So. Fucking. Hot," he gritted, punctuating each word with a shallow thrust.

"Are we okay?" I asked. Ronan nodded and leaned forward to kiss me, the motion sending him deeper inside me. I moaned against his lips and then Zak spoke up.

"Okay, move. My turn."

I laughed and made to sit up when the guys switched, and Zak pushed me back down. His eyes were hard, glittering, like he was angry, but there was a sexy lilt to his lips that made me clench hard again.

"You're a dirty girl, aren't you, Hazel? Letting Ronan fuck you, letting him come inside you. You want my cum too, don't you, baby girl?" he asked, stroking his throbbing cock as I panted.

Oh, damn!

"Don't you?" he pushed, dragging my hips to the edge of the table. Ronan slid his knees beneath my head as Zak had done and gripped my wrists, pulling them up above my head.

"Yes, sire," I whispered. Zak's eyes flashed with arousal, and he grinned.

"I know you do," he murmured and leaned forward to flick his tongue over my clit quickly. I inhaled sharply and he moaned. Judging by the way Ronan's cock jumped beneath me, he liked that too.

"Tell me," Zak demanded. I licked my lips quickly, heat burning hotly in my cheeks.

"I want you to come inside me," I breathed. Zak swore softly and clenched his teeth, his grip on my hips harder.

"I'm going to fuck you, Hazel, and I'm going to come deep inside you. You're going to have two men's cum in your tight little pussy, claiming you, making you ours," he growled.

"Yes," I whimpered, so turned on. "Make me yours."

Zak pressed the head of his raging erection to my opening and paused. I held my breath and then in a swift jerk, he was inside me. Grunting, his eyes rolled back as he slid in easier than he had last night, easier than Ronan had earlier.

"Fuck, you're so wet."

The thought of Zak fucking me with Ronan's cum still inside me was... holy shit, it was hot.

"How does it feel, Zak? How does it feel to fuck her with my cum inside her?" Ronan asked, his voice deep and rough.

"Fucking amazing. Shit, Hazel, you're the perfect woman," Zak moaned, his thrusts coming harder and faster. I closed my eyes and whimpered, my back arching and hips gyrating as I tried to move with him. Ronan leaned over to suck on a hardened nipple, and I cried out again.

"Come on his cock, sweetheart," Ronan whispered as he sat back up.

Zak shifted my legs so that my ankles were flung over his shoulders, sending him deeper inside me. I clawed at Ronan's arms as he held me down with one hand, his other one sliding down to my pussy to circle my clit.

"You like that, baby? You like Ronan playing with your pussy while I fuck you?" Zak asked, his breathing heavy, his eyes dark with desire.

"Yes," I cried out, clenching hard.

"Come for me, Hazel. You're close again, I can feel it," he ground out between gritted teeth, his cock swelling inside me. Ronan's fingers circled my clit faster, harder, Zak groaned and then I was coming again. I cried out and Zak shouted wordlessly as he climaxed. I felt his cum release inside me and it sent another wave of pleasure through me.

Time passed, I don't know how much, but we were all panting and moaning.

"Fucking. Perfect," Zak panted, letting my legs down.

Ronan chuckled and carefully slid out from beneath me. I waited and bit back a moan when Zak pulled out of me. I flushed and wanted to close my legs as both men stared at my pussy, at the evidence of their pleasure and mine on my bare skin.

"Fuck, I want you again," Ronan practically growled.

"Me too," Zak agreed, and I was surprised to see his dick still half hard.

"I can't... not yet," I whispered. The guys smiled and each took one of my hands, pulling me up.

"We'll wait," Ronan assured, leaning forward to brush a kiss over my mouth. I grinned and kissed Zak too, sighing contentedly.

"Let's get you cleaned up," Zak suggested.

I nodded and watched as the guys grabbed their clothes and mine. I didn't bother to try and cover up and laughed when Ronan scooped me into his arms, not allowing me to walk up the stairs. I was going to insist on doing it, but then I remembered what they had said about aftercare, about *needing* to do things like this after sex. It helped them come back to themselves, helped them to ease out of the scene.

I snuggled in closer to his chest and closed my eyes on the warmth in my heart and let my guys take care of me.

CHAPTER SIXTEEN

Three hours later, I was moved out of my hotel room, and all my things—not that there were many—were brought to the guys' apartment.

My guys.

Both of them.

That's right, we'd decided to try out a relationship. Sure, it might be incredibly new and terrifyingly soon, but we all seemed to be on the same page, we were all feeling the same way, so we didn't want to put it off. Somehow, we were all very aware that what we had was rare, and we wanted to make sure nothing got in the way of us keeping it.

A part of me was waiting to go to sleep and wake up in a hospital bed, told I'd had a bad fall and hit my head. The other part of me hoped if that were true, I would never wake up.

Ronan made us dinner, and we talked for hours, getting to know each other better. They asked me a million questions about my life, things we didn't cover earlier in the morning. In turn, I got to learn about both of them and their backgrounds, and I also found out that they were ten years older than me, putting them at thirty-five.

Zak made dessert, and the conversation turned into our favorite and most hated things. They finally explained more in depth about Taylor. I was both pissed off on their behalf and also heart broken.

Eventually we moved onto sexual positions, fantasies, and things we wanted to do. The conversation had gotten unintentionally graphic until we were going at each other right there on the living room floor. I was desperate for them, hungry... and I wanted them both at the same time. After announcing my wish, the guys had seen to it to get me prepared. I'd been in absolute bliss for the last two hours having experienced three orgasms due to their hands, mouths, and the little pink vibrator Ronan used on me to help me stay distracted from the pain of what was currently happening.

I'd never fooled around with back door entry before, and I hadn't expected it to be quite so painful. Then again, that probably had a lot to do with Zak's size as well.

For the last hour they'd been working on me, stretching me, getting me used to the sensation that came with being filled *back there*.

Which was how we'd come to this moment, the moment I'd been wordlessly praying for since the moment Zak had started entering me from behind.

He was *finally* all the way in.

We were sitting in the middle of the large platform bed, me on Zak with my back to him, his legs spread wide and therefore spreading mine, his cock buried deep inside me while Ronan teased my pussy with the vibrator, slipping it in and out to help me feel pleasure over pain.

Zak was shaking beneath me with the restraint it took him not to go hard and fast, not to just fuck me like he wanted to.

"Good girl, sweetheart. Fuck, you're gorgeous," Ronan praised, his voice low and growling after watching Zak stretch me out.

Neither of them moved me, they let me sit and get used to the intrusion. Ronan was pressing the vibrator to my clit, helping me to find the pleasure, while Zak's hands moved to my breasts, cupping them, rolling my nipples and distracting me.

"Okay, green... I think... I think I'm okay," I said after a few long minutes, trying to ignore the burn and focus on the pleasure coming from elsewhere.

Ronan had decided we weren't using a safe word for this activity, but traffic lights. Green meant good, yellow meant slow down or pause, and red meant stop completely. I liked this system.

Zak slowly pulled back a little and rocked inside me. I gasped, the feeling not good, but not awful either. I don't know how long he kept doing this before I felt more accustomed to this position and was able to enjoy the other sensations they were giving me.

"Are you ready for more?" Ronan asked, and I opened my eyes to see him stroking himself. The man was so beautiful.

"Please," I whispered.

"Please what?"

I grinned. "Please, sir."

His dark eyes heated as Zak carefully inched backwards onto the mattress, spreading his legs so that mine spread wider too, keeping me open to Ronan who leaned in close, squeezed my throat, his dark eyes locked on my face.

"You're ours, Hazel."

All I could think was, *God, yes!*

"Color?" Ronan growled, sliding his cock between my folds, lubricating himself with my wetness.

"Green," I gasped, my voice hitching.

With a clenched jaw, Ronan stepped between mine and Zak's spread legs and notched himself at my entrance. It suddenly made sense why they had such a raised bed. Slowly, Ronan eased inside me, and my mouth fell open in a wordless moan, and my head fell back against Zak's shoulder.

"Oh, shit!"

"Hazel?" Ronan gritted out.

"Green, green, green," I said quickly, trying to rock forward but unable to.

"Fuck," he growled and gave a short, sharp, thrust. I arched against him, wincing when it made me more aware of Zak back there.

So. Fucking. Full.

"Green," I mumbled again as he inched forward.

Again and again, Ronan slid deeper, giving me inches of him at a time. I could feel them both, so big, so thick and throbbing. I knew they had to be able to feel each other through the thin membrane that separated them, and somehow that made me ten times hotter.

"Fuck, sweetheart, don't squeeze me like that yet," Ronan snapped, sweat beading on his head as he carefully sank his full length inside me. We were all panting when he stopped, taking a moment to feel it.

"Shit, baby girl. We're both inside your hot little body," Zak groaned, his tone almost reverent.

"You're such a good fucking girl, Hazel. Such a good girl taking both of our cocks. Fucking incredible," Ronan added, rocking his hips slightly.

They both groaned and my moan of pleasure joined theirs when Ronan slid almost all the way out and then thrust back inside me. How was I *ever* meant to have regular sex again? I wasn't sure I'd ever want it vanilla again. I had a feeling that with these two, that would never be an issue.

Slowly, we got into a rhythm where Zak would do a short thrust behind me while Ronan took control in the front. I wasn't allowed to do anything but stay put and let them use my body. And damn, was it the hottest thing I'd ever done in my life. Knowing that these two strapping, hot as hell men were getting off because of *my* body, because of how *I* made them feel, was euphoric. As dirty as it was, as rough and as dominating, I'd never felt more cherished.

"Your body is a fucking paradise, Hazel," Ronan growled, sliding a hand up my chest to my throat again. Zak's fingers continued to strum at my clit, and I could feel myself winding tighter and tighter. Ronan's grip on my throat was strong, and I loved it. I felt full and overwhelmed.

"So perfect. You're such a good girl, making me and Zak feel so good right now, letting us fuck you like this," Ronan grunted, almost trembling with restraint.

"Yes, yes, yes," I chanted, my head falling back as I began to climb that familiar mountain.

"Yes, baby girl, come for us. Let us come inside your hot body together. I want to fill you up with my cum," Zak groaned lowly. Another moan, another groan, and a whimper. The sounds of our heavy breathing, strained cries of pleasure and whispered commands were loud in the room.

"Please, I'm so close," I begged, knowing Zak was keeping my orgasm at bay.

"You're ours, Hazel. Whenever we want you, however we want you, you're ours, sweetheart," Ronan told me, his hips rocking faster and faster against me.

"Yes." I panted.

"Come, baby girl," Zak ordered, his fingers quickening. My breath hitched, my back arched, and my mouth fell open as I *screamed* my release. Holy. Shit!

"Yes!" Ronan roared as he came too, his body shaking.

"Fuck!" Zak cried behind me. I could feel their release, feel the warmth that flooded me from inside as they both rocked and thrusted within me, their combined moans and curses slowly penetrating my pleasure-fogged brain.

None of us moved or spoke for some time, all of us too exhausted, soaring too high.

"Forever, Hazel," Ronan finally said, lifting his head enough to look down at me. His dark eyes were hazy with pleasure and alight with sincerity.

"You're ours, sweetheart. We'll keep you safe, we'll make you happy, we'll do everything in our power to make sure you don't regret your decision to be with us. We'll take care of you. Always," he added, stroking his thumb over my cheek. I blinked slowly, my eyes stinging with unshed tears.

"Promise?" I whispered brokenly.

"We promise," Zak answered, holding me close to him. "You're special, Hazel. We knew that from the first moment we met you, and we're more than certain now. You were meant for us, and we were meant for you."

~

Two hours later, I was curled up against Ronan's chest with Zak pressed up against my back, both their hands stroking my skin as if they couldn't get enough of touching me. I'd soaked in the bath, and just like last time, one of them dried me while the other brushed my hair. They let me touch them both, let me trace their tattoos and run my fingers through their hair. I was exhausted. I ached, but in the most delicious way.

A part of me still expected them to start laughing and tell me I was a fool, that they were joking, and I was so desperate for love and companionship that I'd believe anything. But something about these two men made me feel so damn safe, and I knew in some inexplicable way that I truly was where I was meant to be. Regret at leaving my fiancé never came. Indecision about the life I had chosen to lead was still non-existent. I felt no shame for being with two men, for caring for two men, or for wanting to build a life with them.

Somehow, walking into their bar felt like it was always meant to be, and being around them just felt so damn familiar. Nothing in my life had ever felt more perfect than being wrapped up in their arms or sharing my body with them.

"Ronan?" Zak whispered, his voice low and rumbling.

"I know," Ronan's deep voice replied.

"I know you know. But... goddamn. She's fucking perfect," Zak added. My chest warmed at his praise, and I wanted to cheer, but I was on the cusp of sleep and far too tired to do anything.

"She's ours," Ronan murmured.

"Glad you pulled your head out of your ass long enough to notice."

"Fuck off," Ronan growled, and Zak chuckled behind me.

"We're keeping her, right?" Zak asked softly after a small silence.

"She's not a stray dog, Zakari. But if she wants to be ours, if she really does commit to it, then I won't let her go," Ronan answered softly.

"Glad we agree on that," was Zak's reply.

Feeling like all was right with the world, I let sleep pull me under.

CHAPTER SEVENTEEN

Heaven was the inside of a bar between two tall, dark, and tattooed men.

I knew this to be true because this had been my reality for the past two months. Two months ago today, in fact, when I had walked in on my then-fiancé fucking my best friend in our bed, three weeks before our wedding.

I don't know what force had urged me into my car and onto the highway that led to this town, but I was forever grateful to it. Because of that, I was in a happy relationship with two men who did nothing but worship me and make me laugh. I didn't realize how little I had laughed with Richard until coming here and spending time with these two. Zak was definitely the light-hearted one. He often danced with me in the kitchen or play-wrestled with me in bed. He was always quick with a smile and a dirty joke, and I loved him for that. Ronan was more serious, but so passionate and protective. He made me laugh too, and those times where I got a full belly-laugh from him made me feel fifty-feet tall.

We were happy. Truly and completely.

I mean, no, I wasn't happy with my family. About two days after I had decided to stay here, I called my parents. My father answered, and instead of hearing me out, he went straight to ordering and demanding me to come home, telling me that he was so disappointed in me, and that I was sullying the family name and their good standing by running out on *a good man*. He didn't want to hear what I had to say, he didn't care that I had been hurting or that I had reason enough to stay away. As far as he was concerned, Rich was a great guy and I must have been the one to do something to screw it all up, so I had to be the one to go home to him and apologize. When he wouldn't let me speak, I sucked in a breath and shouted into the phone, "will you shut the fuck up?!"

The silence that had followed should have left me feeling stone dead. I'd quickly apologized for my language but hurried to explain myself. Instead of trying to see things from my point of view, however, he'd told me that he was disappointed, hurt, and that if I cared for him or my momma at all, that I ought to get home right away, or they were going to cut me off. When I reminded him that I had a trust fund with sole access to it, he hung up.

I hadn't heard a thing since. I'd tried calling, but neither of them wanted to hear from me, so in the end, I'd done all I could do. Rich had called a bunch more times, and so had my *ex*-best friend, but I was done with both of them. There was nothing they could say that I wanted to hear.

Richard had gotten his chance, but he'd been more worried about me telling anyone. I didn't care what he had to say now because it was either an apology I wouldn't believe, or he was going to try and convince me to come back and be a good little wife. Either way, I was over it and I had no desire to listen.

As for my friend... it was probably similar to Rich, honestly. I mean, what could anyone say when they had betrayed their best friend in such a brutal way? We'd been friends for fifteen years! Friends didn't do that to each other, and I wasn't sure forgiveness was possible, at least not now. Despite the fact the betrayal of the two closest people to me had led me to my new life, I still couldn't find it within myself to brush it off and let it all go.

So, on the home-front, there was no change.

But here?

I looked around the empty bar and grinned. This was home now, and I loved it. I had hung out more with the women I'd met months ago, Jessie and Steph. They cracked me up, and they always made me feel welcome and cared for. We'd gone out for coffee dates at least once a week, they introduced me to a bunch of their friends who I got along with well, and I'd even gone and had my nails and hair done. I was so glad to have met those ladies, and they were always quick with a compliment or a word of advice where I needed it. They had a million questions about me and the guys, but I was careful what I divulged. Not just because I didn't want any comparisons drawn between me and Taylor, but because I felt like what we did behind closed doors was our business. I wasn't about to go and ask Jess and Steph what their bedroom activities looked like. Although, judging by how well I knew the two women now, they'd likely tell me without a shred of shame or modesty.

I flipped the sign on the door so that it announced we were open and headed back for the office. The guys had given me a job balancing the books and ordering in stock. They realized I had a knack with numbers, and Ronan, for all his god-like abilities, hated computers. As most accounting was done on computers, I'd taken over. I'd taken a few small training courses to familiarize myself with the software, and so far, hadn't had a problem, but I had plans to further my education in this area. Numbers still spoke to me, and I was going to work on improving my skill. When Ronan asked why I didn't do anything with numbers before, I'd explained my mother's theory about math being for boys and he'd mumbled mutinously under his breath. Neither of my guys had said a single bad word to me against my parents despite what they knew of them. They seemed to think it was a bad idea to start bad-mouthing them if we really were going to try and make a go of things.

Everyone else in this town seemed to accept us, and the guys never bothered to hide their affection for me. They were both kissing or hugging me whenever they could, and they loved to dance with me so that the three of us were plastered together on the dance floor. No one so much as raised an eyebrow.

I had truly found my home.

A month ago, we'd gone out on our first official date, and it had been amazing. Again, the guys refused to hide what we were, and so they held my hand all the time or kissed me or touched me. I made sure to do the same with them so they knew I wasn't ashamed or worried about people talking. I had meant what I said to Ronan all those weeks ago; people will talk no matter what. I was tired of living my life according to the advice and rules of others. These men made me inexplicably happy, and I worked hard to make sure they were happy with me.

No one else's opinions mattered.

I was riding that wave of bliss until I heard a voice I never thought I'd hear here in my perfect little world.

Richard.

"I am not going to keep asking, where is Hazel?"

"I don't know who you're talking about," Zak answered in a growl.

Shit.

"Don't play dumb with me. I'm a lawyer; I can spot liars from a mile away. Not to mention several people around here recognized her description and told me she'd been staying here," Richard barked, and I could tell by the tone of his voice that he was about to start throwing his weight around. I shot out of my chair but hesitated before leaving the office, not wanting to see Richard yet if I didn't have to.

"Then they must have been confused. Now leave," Zak demanded.

"Look, I have a friend at the police station. I can make one call and have several officers down here in less than half an hour," Richard snapped.

Yep, there he went. He didn't get his way, so he'd call in the troops.

"Be my guest. Call them," Zak replied, sounding bored.

"You smug bastard. If I find out you've hurt her, there will be nowhere safe for you to hide," Rich snarled.

Sucking in a breath, I hurried out to the bar before anyone could shed blood.

I caught sight of Richard for the first time in months. He still looked the same, but there was no feelings of anticipation or warmth when I looked at him now. He was the same man; tall, broad, and fit. He still had all that thick light brown hair; he wore his usual immaculate suit, and those flashing blue eyes were the same.

But I was different now.

"Richard, that's enough," I cut in.

Three pairs of eyes swung to face me. Zak was standing in front of Richard, keeping him from entering more than the five feet he'd already come. Ronan was by the bar, his arms crossed, and eyes narrowed.

"Hazel, thank Christ," Richard gasped in relief. He tried to make his way toward me, but Zak cut him off.

"Would you tell your attack dog to back off?".

"Zak... it's fine," I assured. After several seconds, Zak stepped aside, but never out of reach, and Richard hurried over to me. Before he could touch me, I held out a hand, stalling him.

"What are you even doing here?" I demanded.

"Me? What are *you* doing here, Haze? Have you *seen* this place?" he shot back.

"I asked first," I fired back.

He frowned and ran his hand over his hair. "I… you haven't returned any of my calls, or Lu's. We've been worried, and your parents aren't saying anything anymore. I needed to make sure you were okay."

I raised an eyebrow and crossed my arms over my stomach.

He groaned and dropped his head back. "Please don't do that."

"Do what?"

"*That*," he said, waving a hand at me. "Don't do that stance and look at me like that. I don't want to fight; I just want to bring you home. Your parents may not be talking about you anymore, but I know they're worried sick."

"No."

"No?" he questioned, looking completely dumbfounded.

"Correct," I answered simply. "It's a two-letter word I'd assume you're familiar with. It means negative. I will not be going with you. I wish you had taken my not answering any calls or texts as a message enough that I don't want to be anywhere near you right now."

"But… why? You have family and friends back home; you have all your things. What do you have here?" Rich pushed.

"What I have is none of your concern. Nothing about me has been any of your worry from the moment I walked in on you with Lu. Actually, no," I cut myself off, thinking better of it. "I stopped being your concern when you *first* cheated on me with my best friend!"

"Haze—"

"No, don't you say my name like that. We are *not* friends, Richard, and I am not someone to be managed. I'm sorry you drove all this way for nothing, but you can leave now. And if you care about me at all, I'd appreciate you not telling my parents where I am. I'm not interested in involving them in my life, and the last thing I need is my father down here demanding I come home or trying to create trouble where there is none," I interrupted.

Richard's eyes slid from me to Zak and Ronan and back.

"I can see where he'd try to make trouble," he murmured in agreement.

"Exactly. Now please... go."

"Haze—"

"She asked you to leave. You need to go. Now."

Zak stepped past Richard and straight to my side where he wrapped an arm around me. I sank against him, and he leaned down to brush a kiss over my head. Richard's eyes widened in realization as he took us in and then he shook his head as if to clear it.

"Hazel... Lu is here in town," he said.

I stilled and anger washed over me. "Lu is here?" I gritted out.

"I know you're mad, but we're both so sorry. Come on, you two have been best friends for over a decade—"

"Which is why this hurt so much!" I cut in. "You two are such assholes. You hurt me worse than anyone else ever has."

"Hazel—"

Zak carefully pulled me behind him and pushed me gently in the direction of Ronan who didn't hesitate to wrap me up in his arms and brush a kiss over my mouth. I relaxed into him and then sighed and turned to Richard.

He gaped at me, his wide eyes swinging from Zak to Ronan and then to me.

"Both of them? You're sleeping with *both* of them?" he gaped.

"Are *you* really going to judge me for who I sleep with? Really?"

I stepped away from Ronan only to have him pull me back again.

Richard's face paled and he took a step back.

"I understand you're hurt, and I understand you won't forgive us. Just..." he trailed off and ran a hand over his head.

"Could you maybe make time to speak to Lu? We're staying at the hotel across the road for the next two nights before we go back. I know we don't deserve it… but maybe speaking to Lu will help you too," he muttered. When I didn't say anything else, he nodded sadly and left the bar.

CHAPTER EIGHTEEN

"Yes, fuck yes, Hazel. That's my girl. Take my fucking cock,"
Ronan grunted, his hand on my throat as he drove into me,
harder and harder. I gasped, rocking my hips against him, feeling
myself careening towards another mind-blowing orgasm.

Zak was watching us breathlessly from the chair beside the bed,
naked and spent. I'd already fucked him, ridden him until he
came. My backside was still throbbing from the riding crop he'd
used, but I loved it. Every red mark was cherished, and I didn't
bother to wonder why it felt that way.

As soon as Zak was done with me, I tackled Ronan, desperate for
more.

Ronan was unleashed tonight, and I think he knew I needed it. I
craved him wild and untamed; I had to have it rough, desperate,
and aching. He was hammering into me without mercy, his grip
on my throat intense, and his grasp on my hip was going to leave
bruises.

I loved every damn minute of it.

Ronan had gone down on me, taken me from behind, and then
fucked my face until tears streamed down my face and I struggled
to breathe. Now, he had me pinned to the mattress, my knees
around his waist as he nailed me without restraint, his hand tight
on my throat.

I scored my nails down his arms, arching my back as he thrust
harder and faster.

"Yes, sweetheart. Mark me. Make me bleed," he groaned, his
voice thick and animalistic. The utter abandon on his face, the
darkness of his eyes, and the gritting of his teeth as he got closer
to the end was breathtaking. We were savage, almost violent

tonight, feeding off one another. He was beautiful in a powerfully masculine way.

I gasped again as I reached that pinnacle and cried out, shattering, totally coming apart around him.

"Yes!" Ronan roared, his head thrown back, his teeth bared and the tendons in his neck standing out.

Utterly. Gorgeous.

We came down slowly, panting and sweating, the world around us spinning and unfocussed. I don't know when he pulled away or when the tears on my face had appeared. I don't know when it was that Zak had cleaned me up with a damp washcloth or when they'd both jumped into bed beside me, wrapping me up tightly and comforting me with their strong, solid bodied. Neither of them spoke; I think they both knew I needed silence. They continued to stroke me, their hands soothing and gentle as I quietly sobbed into my hands.

I could still remember that first year with Richard, how having his attention had been an addiction. I remembered talking to Lu for hours over every little detail. Then a year later, those times I'd talk to Lu about how Rich was distracted, not as affectionate, that he didn't take notice of my haircuts or seem to enjoy our intimate moments. I scrunched my eyes closed when I could clearly recall telling Lu that Rich never even looked at me when we had sex anymore, that he had his eyes closed or he preferred to take me from behind. God! Rich had to have been imagining their times together. He hadn't even been able to look at my face, wishing I were someone else!

Did they get together after and laugh about how naïve I'd been? Did they think it was so funny? Did Lu enjoy telling my fiancé about the times I complained and that I was still so blind to what was in front of me?

I tried not to wonder how often they slept together or how often in the place I slept. It was a struggle not to think about the times they hung out together without me, and I thought it was great, the two most important people in my life were getting along wonderfully.

Hindsight was a bitch.

I concentrated on calming my breathing and stemming my tears. I'd shed enough tears over those backstabbers, enough was enough.

When my crying died off, I wiped at my cheeks and tried to get my breathing under control.

"Did you really love him that much?" Ronan asked softly.

Of course they knew why I was crying. I was grateful because I'd hate for him to think I was crying because he'd gone too far with me. Ronan would never hurt me, not when I didn't want it.

"No," I rasped. "I don't think I ever actually loved him. We were just convenient for each other; we were a perfect match on paper and so we played our parts."

I blinked and shook my head, looking up at the lines on the ceiling rather than at them. It was easier to confess my stupidity when I wasn't staring at them.

"I think—and I know this sounds really shallow—but I think a part of why I am so upset is because of how *stupid* they made me feel. I felt so foolish being tricked by them, so naïve," I admitted.

"That's not shallow," Zak defended.

"And what about your friend?" Ronan asked, as always, hitting the nail on the head.

"Lu," I whispered, my breath hitching.

"Is that betrayal why you're so hurt?" he asked. I nodded, my eyes welling with tears again. I took in a shaky breath and swallowed back my tears.

"We'd been friends since we were ten. Since then, we were pretty much inseparable. We even went to the same college as each other. And... and to know that for three of the four years I was with Richard that they were... that—" I broke off, unable to bite back the sob. The guys wound themselves tighter around me, as if their bigger bodies would be able to shield me from the pain I was feeling.

There was nothing they could do to stop me from feeling the pain of Lu's betrayal. Best friends didn't do that shit to each other.

"Will it make you feel better to talk to them?" Zak asked.

Ronan made a sound of annoyance, and I felt a smile tug at my lips despite my tears.

"She might need to talk to them," Zak defended.

"Look at her. Does it really seem like talking to those backstabbing pieces of shit will help her?" Ronan growled.

"Maybe? I mean, if she gets to yell at them, maybe venting her anger will help?" Zak suggested.

"I don't want her anywhere near them. I don't like it when she cries," Ronan continued as if I weren't even there.

"Maybe the decision isn't up to you," Zak snapped back.

I could feel Ronan preparing to fire another comment at Zak and I pressed a hand to both of their chests.

"Guys, it's fine. Please don't fight about it. Sorry I got all weepy and broke down on you. I guess I was still holding onto a lot of pain and resentment and hadn't properly let myself feel it like I thought I had."

"I don't like you crying," Ronan grumbled, sounding pouty. Chuckling, I leaned over to kiss him.

"I know. Thank you for being so protective," I whispered. Zak cleared his throat dramatically and I laughed, turning to face him.

"I don't like to see your tears either, you know."

"Thank you for trying to give me a chance to do something about all of this. Maybe talking to them will make me feel less powerless in this situation. It's something to consider," I agreed before I leaned up to kiss him too.

We settled into a small silence, and I sighed. "I need a bath."

"I'll get it started," Zak volunteered, rolling off the bed.

"I'll get you a drink," Ronan added and followed.

Grinning, I watched their naked asses leave the room and shook my head. How could I stay upset about anything for long when I had these two amazing men looking out for me?

Hours later, I was curled up in bed with my guys, my head on Ronan's chest with Zak wrapped around me, their body heat enough to keep me warm.

I'd spent a good hour in the tub alone, thinking about my friend, my ex, and my parents. I considered my life and everything it had involved up until now. And I wondered… Where was the blame really meant to land? On my parents to a certain extent, sure. But once I got older, I was the one in charge of my own life and I continued to allow them to dictate my actions and my beliefs. I'd allowed myself to be drawn into the world they'd mapped out for me. And Rich?

No, the way he'd treated me was *not* okay. Cheating on me at all had been a low blow, but to do it with the one friend I'd managed to hold onto throughout my entire childhood?

I could understand their predicament, however. I didn't want to understand, but the problem with still caring about people you knew so well was that you could find ways to stand in their shoes and see it from their point of view.

Rich had used me to escape his reality. We both knew we weren't meant to be. We were content to use each other to play a part and to look good, but neither of us could have ever made each other really happy. I was the person who could complete the image he needed in order to do as society expected with marrying the pretty, docile woman; and I was using him to please my parents and marry the rich husband everyone expected me to be with. We would have grown to resent each other in the end, and we'd have been miserable.

I had been using him just the same way he had been using me. Yes, it sucked he'd gone behind my back and done what he'd done, but really, wasn't I almost as much at fault for our circumstances?

Once I'd come to that conclusion, the humiliation I'd felt at being duped by him faded and I could move on from there. But Lu? That was a betrayal I could *not* see a reason for. I mean, yes, I could see *a* reason, but not one that was good enough.

I'd also pondered that question Zak put forward. Should I go and speak to them and say my piece? Would it help at all? Or would seeing them after that awful betrayal only make things worse?

"You're thinking loudly," Ronan's voice rumbled deeply beneath my ear. "Care to share what's on your mind?"

I sighed and traced the tattoo on his right pec.

"I'm wondering if I should speak to Lu and Rich."

"Do you think that's wise?"

I shrugged. "Maybe not, but I think I'm going to do it anyway."

"I understand speaking to them and getting that betrayal behind you, I just wonder if you're going to face a similar situation later down the road," he pondered.

I frowned. "You think they'll come back?"

"No," Zak piped up, and I smiled. Of course he was awake too. "He's talking about your parents."

Oh.

I studied the swirls and patterns of the tattoo before me and pressed my lips together. I didn't want to consider what I would have to say when I spoke to my parents.

"Why do parents abandon their kids when they turn out different than how they dreamed? Whatever happened to unconditional love?" I asked.

Ronan sighed. "I don't know. No kid of mine will ever be subjected to demands like that. That kind of pressure to be what your parents want and not who you are is damaging in more ways than one."

My stomach flipped at the mention of him having kids and I swallowed hard at the image in my head of a dark-haired little boy with that engaging smile.

"You think about kids?" I asked. His fingers paused where they had been tracing my upper arm and Zak squeezed my hip gently.

"Yes, I want kids someday. I know we haven't had that conversation, but we're still new and I didn't want to scare you away," he answered.

I smiled against him. "Zak?"

"Me too, baby girl. I want kids, as many as my partner is willing to give me," he answered. My stomach swooped, and my cheeks warmed.

"Are we really having this conversation?" I asked, my mind reeling from the sudden change in direction.

"Do you *want* to have this conversation now?" Zak asked instead.

"I... I don't know," I answered, biting back a smile.

"Then that's answer enough for now. But just know we're open to it. Zak and I have talked about this before. Any child by the woman we're with will have two fathers, and we'll be more than happy," Ronan answered.

I snuggled in close, my heart pounding at the thought of carrying a child by these men. I'd wanted kids my whole life; that was the one thing me and my parents could agree on. The future my guys had just given me a glimpse of went a long way to warming me inside where I'd felt cold and raw.

My thoughts turned back to the question Ronan had asked in the beginning and I frowned.

How would that conversation with my parents go? Would they

really abandon me forever? Would my father come looking for me and make trouble? Should I step forward first and try to build a bridge, or was this too big for them to accept?

With a sigh, I curled into Ronan and smiled when Zak pressed a kiss to my shoulder.

I had a sinking feeling that any relationship I had with my parents was well and truly shot now. They were too set in their ways, especially my father. And my mother had been brought up to follow her husband and not have a mind of her own.

No matter what, I would never do to my kids as they had done to me.

That was a certainty.

CHAPTER NINETEEN

It had been a long weekend, but it was finally over. It was two in the morning now, the last of the patrons had been escorted out of the bar and I was stacking chairs onto the tables with Zak.

I was just finishing up when the sounds of raised voices reached us. I frowned and Zak turned with me to face the doors.

"—come here? She said to leave her alone," Ronan growled.

"We need to see her, and we're not leaving until we do." I stalled at the sound of Rich's voice... my ex. He'd found me? I ran a frustrated hand though my hair and sighed, I was not ready for this confrontation, I was happy... but it was here, nonetheless.

"Try to get past me and see what happens. If Hazel doesn't want to see you, then she won't. And you can take your fucking friend with you," Ronan snarled from outside.

I tugged on Zak's hand as we neared the door.

"Just because you're currently putting your dick in her, doesn't give you the right to make decisions for her," another voice snarled, and I felt my stomach hollow.

I knew *that* voice.

There was the sound of a growl, flesh hitting flesh, and a shout. We hurried for the door and found Rich on the ground rubbing his jaw and slowly getting to hit feet. Ronan had another man pinned to the building by his throat, his face a mask of fury.

"Talk about her with that kind of disrespect again, and I'll fucking drop you into a coma, you piece of shit," Ronan threatened, the tone of his voice making me shiver with apprehension. I had no doubt he meant what he said.

"Ronan, let him go," I called, hoping he didn't do damage he'd get into trouble for. Rich was a lawyer after all.

"Not until this fucker apologizes for the way he spoke about you," Ronan growled.

I looked to Zak for help, but he watched at me with a raised eyebrow. "I happen to agree with Ronan."

Throwing my hands up in the air, I huffed impatiently. "Rich, talk some sense into your fucking boyfriend."

"Boyfriend?" Zak asked, frowning.

"Boyfriend?" Ronan echoed, his surprise enough to loosen his grip. The man pinned to the wall stumbled away and held a hand to his throat, gasping.

"What the hell are you doing here, Lu?" I demanded, crossing my arms over my stomach.

Silence followed and then Zak gave a surprised chuckle. "Lu is a guy?"

I nodded, not looking away from the man who had been my best friend for fifteen years.

"Since when do you drop the F-bomb?" Lu asked, straightening up.

"Since now. I'll only ask once more... What the hell are you doing here?"

"Wait... your fiancé cheated on you with your best friend who is a *guy*?" Ronan gaped.

"Can we talk about this later?" I asked with exasperation. Ronan nodded; the amusement was gone from his face.

"We needed to see you, Haze. I wanted to talk to you, to apologize, but you wouldn't answer the phone, and Rich said you had decided to not come home. I had no choice," he defended.

"You could have just left me the hell alone. You're here to soothe your own conscience and considering the pain you have already put me through, it would have been half-way decent if you could have just left me alone."

"I was worried about you," he whispered weakly.

"Oh, so *now* you're concerned with my feelings? What about my feelings for the past three years when you were fucking my fiancé behind my back? Did my feelings worry you at all then? No... because I didn't know, so you could pretend you were a decent human being. You're only here now for your own selfish purposes, and that just proves to me what an asshole you truly are!"

"We never meant to hurt you!" Lu argued, stepping free of Rich's restraining hand. "Fuck, Haze. You know the people we're surrounded by, the stigma and the death threats we'd get if anyone knew."

"And moving never occurred to you?" I returned. "Starting over in a place that was accepting of who you are wasn't an option? No, instead you had to play me for a damn fool and fuck around with *my* fiancé. We have been friends for more than half my life, Lu. And you tossed it all away the day you wanted Rich and didn't tell me," I snarled.

"What would you have done?" Lu demanded angrily. "If I had come to you and said I'd somehow fallen in love with your boyfriend. Oh, and by the way... I'm *gay!*"

"I would have given you my *fucking blessing!*" I shouted; my voice sounded ravaged even to my own ears.

Lu stumbled back and I wiped angrily at the tears on my cheek with the back of my hand. "I loved you, Lu; you were my person. You were my partner in crime, my brother, my best friend, my other half. No matter what else happened in life, you were meant to be the person I could rely on *no matter what.* But you stabbed me in the back, and you made a fool of me every time you went back to Richard for more," I cried, shaking off Zak when he tried to comfort me.

"I'm sorry," Lu whispered, his eyes brimming with tears.

"In all the years we were friends, when did I ever buy into the beliefs of our parents? How many times did we talk about how outdated their views were? How many times did we talk about how we believed it shouldn't matter who you loved, as long as you were a good person?" I pushed, feeling the knife he'd driven into me carve deeper.

Lu's lips trembled, and he looked away, ashamed.

"The worst part, Lu, is that if you had just come to me, and told me how you felt, I would have bowed out. Rich and I had been seeing each other for four years. You two were sleeping with each other for three of those. If you had just said something in the beginning, if you had *trusted* me the way I trusted you..." I trailed off, my breath hitching painfully.

Silence fell between our small group, and I struggled to reign in my tears.

"Haze... I... I wish there was something—"

"There isn't anything you can do, Lu. We're done. No matter what, I'll never be able to look at you and think I can trust you again. There is nothing you can do to make up for the pain you've caused, and the trust you've destroyed," I whispered brokenly, trying to distance myself from the pain.

"Haze—" Rich began, taking Lu's hand. My chest tightened at that simple act, and I ducked my head.

"I get it," I whispered and cleared my throat. "I understand why you both lied. Rich, you're a lawyer, and Lu, you're a doctor. You both hold positions of power in our town. People could destroy your practices easily. I really do understand the need for secrecy, but if you'd just told *me*? Let me in on the secret? I'd have done whatever I could have in order to help the both of you," I confessed, suddenly exhausted.

"We're sorry, Haze. We really are. I wish there was something more we could do or say to make it up to you," Rich apologized. I shrugged.

"It is what it is. There's no going back, and there's no repairing the damage. I've moved on, and I know I am far happier now than I ever was back then. I can only hope you two figure out how to be yourselves and not use anyone else to keep your secret," I replied as Ronan wrapped an arm around me and Zak edged in close, taking my hand in his.

Lu's gaze swept over the three of us, and my heart clenched at that familiar smile on his lips.

"I can see you've got yourself a great thing here. Are you sure it's what you want?" he asked.

"It's better than anything I could have dreamed for myself. And I *am* happy," I answered.

Lu and Rich looked at each other, and I could see the silent conversation, and that they wanted to say more. I wanted to lash out when I realized what it was they wanted to say, but I swallowed it back. Getting mad at them was only draining energy from me. There was literally nothing they could do or say to make me feel better, so having them gone was all that would work. I knew they felt bad, I could see that, but it didn't change anything.

"I'm not going to tell anyone," I gritted out.

Lu's gaze swung back to me, eyes wide and cheeks flushed guiltily.

"Haze—" Rich began, but I held up my free hand.

"I get it. I understand, even if you think I don't, but I have no reason to speak to anyone in that town anymore. And despite how angry and hurt I am, I'm not the kind of person to viciously destroy another. If you knew me at all, you'd know that. Your secret is safe with me, but I really need you both to go now. There's nothing to be gained here but pain for me, and I really want to move on," I cut in, blinking slowly.

They both looked at me, the struggle on their faces apparent.

They knew I was right, and yet they wanted to try, but there was no point. Now all that was left to see was if they would give me the one thing I'd asked for.

After a long, tense, silence, Rich sighed and Lu nodded, brushing away the tears on his face. Seeing his pain still hurt me, but I couldn't get past what he'd done.

"I'll miss you, Haze," he rasped. I blinked away the tears that flooded my eyes and swallowed around the lump in my throat.

"I know, I'll miss you… or the you I thought I knew. I really do wish you both well, and I hope it was all worth it. And I mean that, I'm not just being snarky. I wish you both the best," I added, clearing my throat.

For a moment, it looked like Lu was going to try and hug me, but Rich kept a hold of his hand. Eventually, they both nodded slowly.

"Goodbye, Hazel-Maree," Lu whispered, his lips trembling.

"Bye, Louis. Be safe, Richard," I replied, sucking in a cleansing breath.

With one last look, they both turned around and I watched as they strode across the road to their car. Without looking back, they climbed into their vehicle and drove away.

None of us moved for a long time, and I was grateful that Zak and Ronan let me watch the taillights of their car until it had long disappeared from sight. It hurt to watch them leave, to know we'd said goodbye, and that I would never get that closeness with my best friend again. Lu had been a big part of my life for so long. We'd been together for over half of my life. Saying goodbye, asking him to leave… it hurt. As much as it hurt now, I had a feeling it was going to hurt for a while longer. In the end, this was for the best though.

My heart crumbled a little now that they were gone, but I was glad it was over. The reality was we were done.

Ronan swept his arm around me, and he pulled me into him. I closed my eyes as he held me close, and I breathed in the warmth of him, the scent of him. This was my home now, and I'd never felt freer or more myself. Ronan's fingers tipped my head up and I slowly opened my eyes to meet his gaze. Dark eyes searched my face with that ever-knowing gaze of his. I knew he could see my pain, see my hurt, and my exhaustion. Thankfully, though, he didn't try to placate me with false promises and assurances. Instead, he leaned down and brushed a kiss across my lips.

"I love you," I blurted suddenly. He stilled, and I felt his breath catch. My heart began to pound hard and fast when I realized what I'd just blurted, but I didn't try to take the words back. They were honest, and he deserved to know.

"You love me, sweetheart?" Ronan whispered, almost as if he didn't believe it. I hesitated a moment and licked my lips, but then nodded.

"I do; I think I've loved you for a while," I replied. His dark gaze burned down at me, intense and full of light. My heart was pounding hard in my chest, and I wondered if I'd overstepped, if I'd made a mistake.

"I love you more than you fucking know, Hazel-Maree Connolly. And if there was a way for the two of us to legally marry you, I'd ask you right here right now," Ronan finally answered.

Tears pricked my eyes, and I sucked in a deep breath and grinned.

"Really?"

"Yes, really. Fuck, sweetheart. I've been gone for you since that first night, even though I didn't want to admit it. I love you," he repeated before he kissed me hard. When he pulled away, I to Zak and he wrapped me up in his arms.

"Me too, baby girl?" he asked, cupping my face, his expression softening.

"Of course, you too, Zakari. I love you so damn much," I whispered. His face lit up and my heart pounded hard at the look of adoration on his face.

"Good. I love you too, baby girl. Like Ronan said, I wish we could both marry you because I'd do it right here and now. I never thought we'd find someone like you; never dreamed of someone so amazing," he answered.

I laughed shakily and a tear escaped my blurry eyes. Zak brushed it away with his thumb and leaned in to kiss me deeply. I kissed him back, hard, loving the way these men gave everything to me so freely.

"Come on, baby girl. Let's get you upstairs," Zak said softly. Ronan took my other hand, and together we shut the door and locked up. I was in love with two incredible guys. And what was more? They were both in love with me too.

Even better... I didn't have to choose between them.

EPILOGUE

One Year Later...

Closing the doors after the lunch rush was over, I ran back up the stairs to the apartment.

I sent Zak and Ronan out on a small shopping run an hour ago, and they'd be back any minute. It was time to get things in order; I wanted to have their surprises ready for when they got here.

I looked around our home and smiled. It had changed a lot over the last year that I'd been here, and it was more of a home for the three of us now. The guys didn't protest too much about my feminine touch, as long as I left the gaming consoles and the giant TV where they were, they were happy for me to make it mine as well.

I'd read their books on BDSM and then devoured their small collection of female erotic romance books. I'd become obsessed and extensively added to what was there.

A year. A whole year.

If someone had told me two years ago what my life would look like now, I would have snorted and laughed hysterically. Never in my wildest dreams did I ever think I'd be living with and in love with two men at the same time... and that they'd be *happy* about the arrangement.

Every week was a new lesson with these two. Just when I thought I'd learned everything there was about sex with two men, a relationship with two men, dominance and submission and the *true* meaning behind the lifestyle, I was proven wrong. There was so much, but it all strangely felt natural. I knew my guys; I knew what they needed and when they needed it.

And if me kneeling before them with my hands raised, palms up, and my head down gave either of them a sense of calm or power, then I was happy to do it for them. Honestly, it was so empowering for me too. I know, it was weird to think being bound and gagged or tossed around like a rag doll would be freeing, but it was... and it was *oh, so delicious.*

I turned toward our bedroom and went straight to the drawer in the corner. I had a present made up for them last week, and I wanted to give it to them today.

I had just put my hands on the twin boxes when I heard the apartment door open and close.

"Baby girl?"

"Sweetheart?"

Their voices rang out at the same time, and I grinned. They always called me those two names. Or princess, and sometimes kitten.

I quickly snatched the boxes out of the drawer and had just hidden them behind my back when they entered.

They paused in the doorway and looked at me with suspicion.

"What are you doing?" Ronan asked, his gaze traveling over me. I knew I looked guilty; I could never hide anything from these guys and now was no exception.

"Nothing."

Zak looked at Ronan and then at me, an eyebrow raised, a spark of excitement in his eyes.

"Oh, really?" Zak asked, slowly putting down the shopping bags in the doorway. I swallowed hard, anticipation rising within me. My skin tingled and my core throbbed. I knew those looks, I knew what it meant, and my body was raging for it.

"Truly," I answered.

"Sweetheart, you're a terrible liar," Ronan informed me, slowly stepping forward. The move was languid, fluid, predatory. My breath hitched and my nipples peaked.

"I was just getting something out of my drawer," I answered.

"Oh?" Zak asked, mirroring Ronan's step.

I nodded, licking my lips nervously.

"You know what happens if you're caught lying to us, don't you, baby girl?" Zak murmured.

"I'm not lying," I whispered.

"Lying about lying will get you punished even worse," Ronan growled, and a shiver went down my spine. I stepped slightly to the side, towards the bed, planning to jump over it and then down the side towards the hall. I'd have to be quick.

"You'll have to catch me first," I said quickly and then bolted towards the bed. I saw them both move, lunge for me, but I rolled over the massive platform bed and hit the ground on the other side with both feet. I was moving again before either of them reached the bed, dodged Zak, and *barely* escaped Ronan's long grasp before I zipped out the door. A laugh bubbled up as I ran out the door, the two small boxes still clutched in my hands. I could hear them running behind me, their larger bodies slightly slower than mine. Skidding to a halt once I reached the living room, I spun to face them. I was breathing heavily, but it was from excitement more than exertion.

"Nowhere to run," Zak murmured as he edged closer.

"Nowhere to hide," Ronan finished.

I licked my lips again and Ronan made a sound deep in his chest, like a growl.

"Kneel, princess. Show us how sorry you are for lying," Zak ordered. My entire body was alive with awareness and my breasts felt heavy. Heat pooled low, and I struggled not to squeeze my thighs together.

"Kneel," Ronan repeated, his voice thick.

Biting back a groan, I slowly sank to my knees before them, keeping my eyes up. When I was finally lowered, I slowly bowed my head, my eyes downcast.

"Hands, baby girl."

My heart pounding hard, I held my breath as I slowly raised my hands palm up, a small white box in either hand.

Silence was loud around me for a moment.

"Baby?" Zak questioned. I didn't move, I didn't speak, I just waited. One at a time, I felt them take the boxes out of my palm and I waited some more.

"Sweetheart," Ronan whispered huskily.

"Baby girl?" Zak repeated, also deep and rough.

"Hazel… look at us."

I wanted so badly to see them, to know how they looked, to take in their expressions, but I was also nervous.

"Hazel," Zak whispered.

Sucking in a breath, I slowly raised my gaze to find each of them holding a silver band in their hands. Neither were looking at them though, their eyes only for me, full of love, heat, and hope.

"I… I know we can't legally get married," I began shakily. "But I thought maybe, if you two agree, if you want to… we could have a union ceremony. Something that works for the three of us, and we can invite our friends to be a part of it," I explained, my hands shaking as I lowered them.

"You…" Zak trailed off, swallowing hard, his eyes straying back to the ring.

"What's this?" Ronan asked, bringing the ring closer to his face. I smiled and waited.

I'd had the words *Forever & Always* engraved on the inside of his ring. Zak had *Always & Forever*.

"I wanted it to be more than just a ring," I answered. Zak studied his ring, and I watched their faces fill with several emotions, expressions fleeting and chasing one another.

"Stand up, sweetheart," Ronan whispered. I got to my feet

shakily and Ronan stepped forward, tugging on my hand to bring me against him.

"I love you, Hazel-Maree. And it would be my honor to have a union ceremony with you," he rasped. I grinned and leaned up to kiss him. He made it slow, languid, claiming. When we pulled away, I was breathing heavy, and I watched with deepening joy as he slid the ring onto his ring finger.

"Baby girl," Zak whispered, tugging me over to him. He framed my face with both of his hands, his dark eyes searching my face, his gaze like a soft touch.

"We became the luckiest men in the world the night you came into our bar. I fell for you that night and I have been falling ever since. I love you, baby, and I can't wait to put a ring on your finger," he whispered. Grinning, I blinked as my eyes stung with unshed tears. Dipping his head, Zak claimed my mouth and kissed me slow and deep.

I pulled back a small time later and watched as he too slid his ring on. I looked from one man to the other and felt a deep sense of belonging wash over me.

Zak looked at Ronan and he nodded, and Zak left the room. I frowned and opened my mouth to ask what was going on when he came back and handed Ronan a small box similar to the one I'd given them.

"We got you something," Ronan explained. My heart leapt in my chest, and I reached out with a shaking hand as Ronan handed me the box.

I flicked a glance at both of them to find them watching me with apprehension. Slowly, I opened it and gasped at the white-gold band. Actually, it was two bands, but they had been fused together. I pulled it from the velvet cushion and looked at it carefully. There were gentle engravings on the top, swirls and patterns that were so delicate it was amazing it was even possible to put on a ring.

"There's an inscription," Zak announced. I looked inside and grinned, my eyes misting over.

Ours to keep.

"Will you be, Hazel?" Ronan asked.

"Ours? Forever?" Zak finished.

I nodded and laughed, slipping the ring on my left ring-finger.

"Yes, of course," I agreed shakily. The guys wasted no time in hugging me, pulling me between them, kissing me wherever they could. I soaked in the moment, the feeling of being between my guys and drawing them into my lungs.

This was what true happiness was right here.

"We need to find a new place," Ronan stated, pulling away suddenly.

"I was just thinking that," Zak added with a quick nod, stepping back slightly.

"There's that three bedroom down on main street," Ronan suggested.

"Three? No, we'll need more room than that. I'm sure we could speak to Lindy at the real estate, and she'll find us somewhere bigger and quieter," Zak replied, shaking his head.

"Wait, bigger? Why? What's wrong with here?" I asked, a part of me hating the idea of leaving the room above the bar.

"Baby... I know we only spoke about it briefly a year or so ago," Zak began, brushing his thumb over my cheek.

"But we're ready to get our lives started, and we're definitely going to need the space," Ronan added.

"What..." I trailed off, but then it clicked. I sucked in a sharp breath and tried to suppress the thrill that ran through me.

"You mean, you guys want to start trying for kids?" I asked hopefully.

"I can't imagine anything more beautiful than you barefoot and pregnant with our babies," Ronan groaned, leaning in to kiss me quickly.

"You mean it?" I whispered, wanting to be a mother more than anything.

"Absolutely," they said together. I grinned and looked at them both with such love. There they stood, my guys, wearing my rings and talking about our kids... our family.

A girl could die of happiness.

"First, we're doing this union ceremony," Zak reminded.

"Of course, but there's something else we need to do before that," Ronan agreed.

"What?" I asked, confused.

They both turned to look at me, and the minute they did I knew what they wanted, what we needed. A shiver ran down my spine and my lower abdomen flipped in anticipation.

"Run, sweetheart," Ronan warned, his voice low and eyes glittering with heat.

"We'll give you to the count of three," Zak added.

"Yes, sir. Yes, sire," I replied immediately. I watched their expressions heat and their bodies tense ever so slightly.

"Good girl," Zak praised softly, his voice a deep rumble of approval.

"One," Ronan began.

I ran for the bedroom, my heart hammering, my grin wide and my body on fire, readying for the pleasure it was about to receive.

I loved being their good girl.

THANK YOU FOR READING

HER SIR & SIRE

Her Sir & Sire was originally a part of a BDSM anthology and when the rights were returned to me, I brought it out as a steamy standalone romance with bonus content that I'd previously had to cut out.

Thank you for reading and I truly hope you enjoyed! If you're feeling brave, check out the other books written by me!

DID YOU KNOW...
I HAVE TWO OTHER PEN NAMES?

I know that seems like overkill, but there is a method to my madness.

Books under the name **Alexis Maree** are for paranormal romances. Not everyone likes to read this genre, so I like to keep them separate.

Likewise, not everyone likes contemporary romances, so I have another pen name for those...**T. Maree**.

Then last, but certainly not least, are my sinfully sexy romances, the ones that border on the line of *"should she really put that down in print?"*
Some people don't like those kinds of spicy scenes, and so I decided to keep those separate from the rest under the name **Luna Maree**.

So, if you'd like to check out what else I've written, go onto my website

Happy reading!

Alexis | Luna | T.spell

ABOUT THE AUTHOR

DID YOU KNOW...
I HAVE TWO OTHER PEN NAMES?

I know that seems like overkill, but there is a method to my madness.

Books under the name **Alexis Maree** are for paranormal romances. Not everyone likes to read this genre, so I like to keep them separate.

Likewise, not everyone likes contemporary romances, so I have another pen name for those...**T. Maree.**

Then last, but certainly not least, are my sinfully sexy romances, the ones that border on the line of "*should she really put that down in print?*"
Some people don't like those kinds of spicy scenes, and so I decided to keep those separate from the rest under the name
Luna Maree.

So, if you'd like to check out what else I've written, go onto my website.

Happy reading!

Alexis | Luna | T.

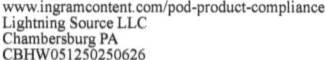